Elgar: The Erotic Variations
AND
Delius: A Moment with Venus

D1287963

By the same author
Beethoven Confidential and *Brahms Gets Laid*
   (also published by Peter Owen)
Altered States: The Autobiography of Ken Russell
A British Picture
Directing Films
The Lion Roars: Ken Russell on Film
Mike and Gaby's Space Gospel
Revenge of the White Worm
Violation

Elgar:
The Erotic Variations

AND

Delius:
A Moment with Venus

KEN RUSSELL

PETER OWEN

LONDON AND CHESTER SPRINGS, PA, USA

PETER OWEN PUBLISHERS
73 Kenway Road
London SW5 ORE

Peter Owen books are distributed in the USA by
Dufour Editions Inc., Chester Springs, PA 19425-0007

First published in Great Britain by Peter Owen Publishers 2007

ISBN 978 0 7206 1290 5

A catalogue record for this book is available from the British Library

Printed and bound in Great Britain by
Windsor Print Production Ltd, Tonbridge, Kent

For Elize and in memory of Eric Fenby –
and with special thanks to Simon Yeadon

Preface

I'VE MADE FIFTEEN biographical films on composers to date and have come to the conclusion that most of them have a dual personality – something I call the 'Dr Jekyll and Mr Hyde' factor. And this is no more evident than in the cases of my two best-loved English composers, Frederick Delius and Sir Edward Elgar.

Both were provincial lads whose fathers were in trade, were largely self-taught and after years of struggle finally found fame in Germany before achieving recognition in the land of their birth. How different to their aristocratic and titled English contemporaries who could only churn out third-rate Brahms and were nevertheless all the fashion. Delius and Elgar were different – their music was uniquely English, though their individual styles were as different as chalk and cheese; or, perhaps I should say, heart and soul. But talent will out, and over seventy years since their deaths in 1934 they are still top of the Brit classical pops.

It was in the early 1960s when making drama-documentaries for the BBC Arts programme *Monitor* that I had the great opportunity to bring Elgar, my favourite composer, to the attention of thousands of viewers who up until then had been unaware of his genius. Until that historic moment, which heralded the great Elgar revival, most of the critics had contrived to belittle his unique spirit, his compassion and his ability to capture in music that elusive spirit that makes Britain great – not only the obvious, pomp-and-circumstance sort of thunder (though there's no denying that he could produce this with knobs on) but, more subtly, something special in the very air we breathe that is peculiar to these islands: an inheritance permeating our blood, body, bones and mind. And this is what I tried to show, too, in my second film on Elgar – made forty years later in colour and stereo sound for Lord Bragg's *South Bank Show* for Independent Television.

The original black-and-white BBC film was a straightforward cradle-to-the-grave affair featuring the Malvern hills as Elgar's major inspiration, while the new version featured music associated with his wife and friends. Even so, by their very nature, these films were highly pictorial, and there was little opportunity to delve below the surface of this complex man with the persona of Colonel Blimp and the passion of a Don Juan. My biography presented here is the private man revealed by half a century's research and, more importantly, by consulting of the magic crystal ball of his music.

A few years after making the Elgar film for *Monitor* the producers asked me to make a second based on Frederick Delius's last years, *A Song of Summer*. After gathering dust for many years in the vaults at the BBC, this, together with the Elgar film, is now available on videocassette and DVD, and, with the renewed interest, I realized that another of my favourite composers has been haunting my thoughts again.

And as was the case when I first made my drama-documentary for the BBC arts programme in the late 1960s, my evangelical spirit has very much been brought to the fore once more. But another film on the composer is out of the question. For one thing, arts programmes on television are not what they used to be. And now that Max Adrian is no longer with us there is no one around who could replace him in the leading part he made his own. So, instead, I've tried a different approach, one that I hope is equally accessible and involving. I've attempted to produce a word-picture of what comes to mind when a Delius recording is playing, instead of an image on the box. Of course, I've given my favourite pieces of music pride of place. In doing so I hope that I have not only given a hint of the mood of the music itself but conveyed, too, something of the composer's colourful life – both documented and those elements that could only be speculated on.

Much of this material will be new to the reader – including the fact that Frederick was actually baptized 'Fritz' – for which, in the main, I have to thank my friendship with Eric Fenby, Delius's amanuensis. During the making of my film and indeed for some considerable time after, I spent many enjoyable hours with Eric, who shared a treasure trove of fascinating memories not generally known to the world concerning the fancies and foibles of the cantankerous old genius, and for which I am most grateful. Eric was an unassuming man who sacrificed his own composing career to further that of a talent he felt was far greater than his own. He had great charity of spirit.

At any rate, having made award-winning films on both Elgar and Delius and relished their music for many years I felt I should pass on their intriguing secrets – perhaps to help their fans appreciate them even more – while I still have the chance. And if I've got any aspects wrong (perish the thought), I hope they'll have the opportunity to put me right some day.

Elgar:
The Erotic Variations

Contents

ELGAR: THE EROTIC VARIATIONS

ONE	The Odd Couple	15
TWO	The Unconventional Wedding Night	20
THREE	Consummation	25
FOUR	When Knights Were Bold	30
FIVE	Wandering Lonely as a Cloud	36
SIX	The New Woman	38
SEVEN	Bon Mots	43
EIGHT	Carice Speaks Out	50
NINE	True Confessions	57
TEN	Post Mortem	61
ELEVEN	A Bicycle Built for Two	66
TWELVE	The Peerage Postponed	72
THIRTEEN	Sir Ted	76
FOURTEEN	Nobilemente	81
FIFTEEN	Five Stars	84
SIXTEEN	Undesirable Aliens	88
SEVENTEEN	Requiem	94
EIGHTEEN	The Pilgrimage	99
NINETEEN	The Same Coin	105
TWENTY	The Last Muse	114
TWENTY-ONE	A Daughter's Revenge	120
TWENTY-TWO	The Last Laugh	125

ONE

The Odd Couple

S HRIEKS, SCREAMS, CLOUDS of billowing steam and cries of the damned. To Elgar, a boyish thirty-year-old, it was Dante's Inferno and he was right in the middle of its whirling vortex. Rather pleased with the allegory, he sought to impress his matronly travelling companion by passing it on.

'This is like Dante's Inferno, don't you think?' he shouted above the unearthly din.

'Very like indeed,' said his companion, whose name was Alice Elgar.

They were husband and wife, and this was the first day of their honeymoon.

'A metropolitan station of this magnitude with not a single porter in sight is indeed hell,' she continued.

Elgar smiled. Though their perceptions were quite different they had arrived at the same conclusion.

They were referring to Waterloo Station in the early-morning rush-hour of 9 May 1889. Elgar was quite overwhelmed. With thirteen platforms it was by far the largest station he had ever seen – his home town of Worcester had but two. Alice, on the other hand, had passed this way on more than one occasion – always with a fleet of servants, so in that respect this was a new experience for her, too.

'Where to?' shouted a porter, appearing out of the blue.

'Southampton,' replied Elgar, raising his voice above the hubbub.

'Central or Terminus?'

'I'm afraid I've no idea,' said Elgar, turning to Alice for guidance.

'We wish to connect with the Red Funnel Service to Ventnor on the Isle of Wight,' she replied imperiously. 'It sails from the Royal Pier.'

'Thank you, madam,' the porter replied, respectfully touching his cap and starting to load his trolley. 'You'll be needing the Terminus then.' After which he set off at such a pace that they had to break into a trot to keep up with him, Alice's dainty heels beating a fastidious staccato on the ground.

'First class, I presume,' said the porter over his shoulder to Alice.

'*Naturellement.*'

'*Mercy*,' replied the porter, illustrating that a little knowledge is a dangerous thing.

Impertinent fellow, thought Elgar. He's completely ignoring me.

Too true, the porter knew very well on which side his bread was buttered, thank you very much. It was simply a question of diction and dress. The bloke spoke like a country bumpkin and wore a Sunday-best suit that would have been the laughing stock of Savile Row. The lady, on the other hand, was definitely out of the top drawer, even if she was a bit hoity-toity. And that pearl choker must be worth a bob or two. No doubt who held the purse strings in that little set-up.

And so it proved – when he wished her a *bon voyage* and had a coin dropped into his hand. Elgar he continued to ignore. The things some men will do for money, the porter thought as he touted for his next customer. And she old enough to be his mother!

A keen observer of human character, the porter was close to the mark in some respects but way off in others.

For one thing, Elgar was not a gigolo. There was barely nine years' difference in their ages, though it must be admitted that the noonday sun of the tropics had not smiled kindly on dear Alice, giving rise to the erroneous but widely held belief that she was well on the wrong side of forty.

But, as the train chugged out of the station and Elgar gave her a hearty kiss through her veil, she was sweet sixteen again.

They sat side by side, holding hands as the countryside sped by and spent the next ninety minutes comparing it unfavourably with their beloved Malvern Hills. That was where their courtship had blossomed, while they grew ever more intoxicated drinking the waters at St Anne's Well and taking steep donkey rides up to the Beacon.

Then it was all hustle and bustle from Southampton Terminus to the Royal Pier, where the twin-funnel paddle steamer the *Pride of Hampshire* awaited their pleasure. And pleasure it was for both of them as they leaned on the rail and chugged down Southampton Water toward the island that Queen Victoria had, by her occasional presence at Osborne House, lifted from the depths of obscurity to the heights of snobility.

Alice was thrilled to have a young man's arm around her waist (for the first time in her life). Elgar was thrilled by the power of the gleaming steam engine throbbing away beneath his feet, propelling him towards a new world where the little creature at his side would be his guide. It was she who had suggested their present destination, and there it was, slowly materializing through the mists ahead of them – the Isle of Avalon, calling King Arthur and his queen to make it their very own, at least for a fortnight, at the Seaview Private Hotel, 25 Clifftop Terrace, Ventnor. And that is the address they gave the cabby on landing.

The distance from the pier to their destination was little over a hundred yards, which surprised them.

'If I'd known it was that close, we could have walked and saved the fare,' Alice remarked on their arrival.

'Indeed we could have,' grinned Elgar, 'if you'd married a Strong Man from the circus. I'm used to carrying nothing heavier than a violin, my love.'

'Naturally, I didn't mean you to carry the luggage all the way up the hill, Edu,' she replied with a wan smile. 'We could have sent the porter down from the hotel to collect it.'

'I very much doubt this "hotel" has a porter,' said Elgar, taking in a modest guest-house, indistinguishable from an entire terrace of modest guest-houses. By now the cabby had unloaded their luggage and was giving Alice a helping hand to terra firma.

But Alice refused to be downhearted, and where Elgar saw only a drab little dwelling she saw a romantic little love nest. What matter if her spectacles were rose tinted? They had stood her in good stead throughout their entire courtship, whenever the family had put obstacles in the way.

He was 'socially inferior'. He was 'a Catholic, stinking of incense'. He was 'after her money,' they chimed.

She'd show them. She'd win him a knighthood. She'd convert to Catholicism herself. She'd make him rich.

'Thank God your parents are dead and buried,' her tormentors chorused. 'It would have killed them.'

Unable to weaken her resolve, they resorted to spite and cut her off without a penny. But Alice had inherited a modest sum from her parents' estate – just enough to tide them over until Edu came into his own, so she was not unduly worried. The future was theirs for the taking.

From somewhere behind doors on that cobbled sea-view street a bell sounded. For Alice it seemed to signify the end of 'round one' in a contest she could hardly name – a round she confidently felt she'd won on points.

To celebrate her triumph, she added a threepenny bit to the cabby's fare.

The landlady and a scullery boy helped them drag their luggage up a flight of narrow stairs to the 'first-floor front', where Alice collapsed into a shabby armchair. The news that they had just missed dinner was hardly the welcome she'd hoped for. Neither was the announcement that a cold collation awaited them downstairs, when they were ready – 'but not too late, please, as the maid has to set the tables for breakfast'. Not only did Alice dislike being spoken to thus by inferiors but blancmange was one of her least favourite desserts, despite its Gallic connotations. So, altogether, she was not best pleased.

Elgar, too, was feeling a little low but whistled a merry tune as he started to unpack his well-worn suitcase, plonking down on Alice's portmanteau to do so. But, conscious of her mood, he made an effort to cheer her up.

'Why don't we go out for a bit of supper, old girl?' he said, swivelling around and taking her hand. 'I noticed a cosy-looking pub opposite the pier. What do you say?'

Alice inwardly winced at the 'old girl' but nevertheless was grateful for Elgar's solicitude.

'You are sweet,' she replied, squeezing his hand, 'but unless you are absolutely ravenous I'd be quite happy to forgo supper and retire sooner than later.'

Elgar inwardly winced at the word 'Edu'. It was a diminutive of the name Eduard, which was the German equivalent of Edward. Why couldn't she call him that and be done with it, or Ed or Eddie or even Teddy? After all, he was British and proud of it. A true patriot. But so was Alice, come to that, and unlike Elgar had a pedigree to prove it. Her father, Sir Henry G. Roberts, Knight Commander at the Bath, had served Queen and Country in the capacity of Major-General in command of the Bombay native light infantry.

By contrast, Elgar's dad was nothing but a humble shopkeeper and piano tuner, admitted to stately homes only through the back door, and told to remove his shoes and don gloves before entering the music rooms of the nobility, such as the General. The same had applied to young Edward on the occasions when he assisted his father, he recalled with an involuntary shudder. And that same code of conduct had still been the norm many years later, when he called to give Alice lessons on the violin.

It was in that gracious setting, where he was such an awkward guest, that the lady of the house progressed from a growing affection for her handsome music teacher to the firm conviction that she would eventually marry him. And it is much to Alice's credit that she had the tenacity and strength of character to break the bonds of convention that had bound her from birth.

No one appreciated this more than Elgar himself. He was willing to forgive her anything. Even that despicable nickname Edu.

'So, what do you say, Edu?' Alice said, breaking Elgar's train of thought and bringing him back to the here and now. 'Are you as ready for bed as I am?'

For an answer, Elgar kissed her on the lips, kicked off his boots and made an effort to gear himself up for a night of passion. But Alice had not finished. 'I don't know about you, my love, but, for the life of me, I can never recall being so dead, dead tired.'

At this Elgar mentally breathed a deep sigh of relief . Reprieved!

TWO

The Unconventional Wedding Night

*T*HEY HAD BEEN married the day before at Brompton Oratory – a fashionable Catholic church in South Kensington. The few friends who attended the ceremony were also invited to a wedding break-fast, given by the only aunt to have stood up for Alice at her little house in nearby Drayton Gardens.

Like the bride and groom the guests had come from opposite ends of the social scale; so, to begin with, conversation had been limited to the weather. But by the time that old reliable standby had been mangled and hung out to dry a considerable amount of alcohol had been consumed, so everyone departed in good spirits.

The ensuing wedding night had been unconventional, to say the least, with Alice doubling up with the maiden aunt and Elgar making the best of a lumpy settee. Had they married at home things would have been different, but they had needed to make an early start in the morning and hotels in London were expensive, so economies had won over convention. It had been a sacrifice they were both willing to endure in the circumstances.

And when they awoke on the second morning of their marriage to the screaming of gulls Alice was still a virgin – and a hungry one at that. Even before Elgar had time to yawn, she was out of bed and splashing cold water on her face.

An hour later they were all dressed up and walking briskly along the front, where early birds of all ages were frolicking in sand and surf. They were then challenged by a steep winding hill, which took some of the wind out of Alice's sails, causing her to turn and admire the view frequently, until with the support of her trusty parasol and Elgar's firm grip on her elbow she finally reached the summit.

Immediately the sight of the imposing Royal Hotel confronted them, putting their present accommodation to shame.

'Thank heavens we didn't go there,' Alice frowned, catching sight of a group of guests being assisted into a variety of splendid conveyances. 'They look unspeakably *nouveau riche*.'

'And there's no doubt who's got the best view,' replied Elgar non-committally, for, to tell the truth, he was just a bit envious.

Turning left, they walked along Undercliff Drive. After passing the miniature golf course – 'We must have a round there some time, Edu' – they soon arrived at the Botanical Gardens, as the local council had chosen to rechristen the municipal park.

They took their seats at the bandstand, where the morning concert was already in progress. Pot-boilers mostly, with an attractive selection of waltzes and polkas by Johann Strauss. But if they'd waited for the Medina Marching Band to play one of Elgar's lighter pieces, such as Sevilliana or Serenade Mauresque, they would have been old and grey. Which is a pity, because those attractive miniatures would by no means have been out of place rubbing shoulders with those by the King of the Waltz. As it was, they had been taken up by local bands around Worcester, where they had been very well received.

Reading a tinge of regret on Edu's countenance, Alice leaned across and whispered in his ear. 'When we come back for our silver wedding anniversary it will be Edward Elgar all the way. Mark my words.'

Elgar returned her optimistic smile but felt nowhere near as confident. Already into his thirties and still only a local talent, he wondered if there would ever come a day when his music would be played in every bandstand in the land. He doubted it. To make his mark he needed to write a big work with international appeal. And if the great names of the day, such as Sir Arthur Sullivan, Sir Granville Bantock, Sir Hubert Parry and Sir Frederick Bridge, couldn't really make it, what chance did plain Mr Elgar have?

Well, even if international fame was out of reach he'd be happy to settle for a little recognition in Germany. What a tradition! Bach, Beethoven, Brahms, Wagner and now the up-and-coming Richard Strauss. His dream was to have his music taken up by the greatest living conductor in the world today, Julius Buths. There, German again!

Maybe Alice was right, maybe the Germanic 'Eduard' would produce better results, but it hadn't helped the very British Sir Edward German, had it? And the idea of Germanizing the very British 'Elgar' was ludicrous. No, he was English through and through, and that would be true of every note of his music. But if foreigners could take Shakespeare to their hearts, why not Elgar?

'Fancy eighteen holes, darling?' said Elgar to Alice as they passed the miniature golf course on their return journey.

'Not at the moment, Edu, but after a judicious repast, perhaps.'

They were in sight of the Royal Hotel, which prompted Elgar to ask, 'How about a bite at the Royal, darling?'

Alice was getting somewhat weary of the word 'darling', which she associated with the degrading vocabulary of the *parvenu*, which, in turn, she associated with the four-star hotel dominating the view. Besides, it would be expensive – which was, of course, only of secondary importance, she told herself.

'Did you notice that charming hostelry at the bottom of the hill, Edu? I'm sure it would be far more convivial.'

And far cheaper, Elgar thought, uneasy at the prospect of the penny-pinching existence opening up before him. She wasn't that hard up, surely? Or was she? He wondered.

'Good idea,' he replied with enthusiasm, as was his habit with most of Alice's suggestions.

But sitting at a wooden table on the pub terrace that overlooked the Channel, savouring a Dover sole and a bottle of Chablis, he had no reason at all to regret his false enthusiasm. Alice, too, seemed at peace with the world, as she toyed with her veal escalope à la Ventnor. For a while, conversation took a back seat as they basked in the warm sun, relishing their food and listening to the cry of the gulls and the sound of the wavelets gently breaking on the rocks below.

And as Elgar relaxed thoughts of his last visit to the seaside came to mind. Cornwall – Lizard Point, which was as close as you could get to New Zealand without actually taking leave of these shores. It was still a long way to go, but Elgar got as close as he could, scrambling down the rocks until he was in danger of getting his boots wet.

His exceptional prowess as a fielder in the Worcester Musicians' Cricket Club came into play. With tremendous force he hurled the bottle he had been gingerly handling further out to sea than seemed humanly possible – or so it appeared to a group of curious tourists, who broke into spontaneous applause on witnessing the feat.

Elgar ignored them – the sight of a grown man with tears in his eyes might have troubled those curious bystanders had he turned to acknowledge them. Besides, it was none of their business, so he stood there gazing out at the receding bottle, his mind full of memories.

'A penny for them,' said Alice, snapping him out of his reverie.

'Er, well . . . to tell the truth, I was thinking about music,' said Elgar, getting away with a half-truth before quickly changing the subject.

'Now, what would you like for afters, my sweet?'

I really will have to take his vocabulary in hand, Alice thought, and not for the first time. Aloud, she said, 'A dessert, ah, yes, why not? Let's indulge ourselves. I'd like a Cointreau sorbet. How about you?'

'Treacle tart for me, I fancy,' said Elgar after scanning the menu. 'But I don't see any mention of Cointreau . . . what was it, my love?'

Alice suppressed a frown. 'Sorbet. It's a digestive, a water ice.'

'Ah, you want a water ice,' laughed Elgar. 'Why didn't you say so in the first place, dearest?' And he bounded up the stairs to the public bar to place his order.

Alice was mildly piqued and speculated on how long she would have to work on him before he was sufficiently groomed to be accepted into polite society. Obviously she would have to tread warily, and it would take time; but hopefully not too much time, for at thirty-nine she was hungry for fame and fortune.

Further speculation was cut short by Elgar's buoyant return.

'No "sore bay",' he quipped, making fun of the foreign word. 'They never heard of it. So here's the next best thing. A nice vanilla ice, best Devonshire, with a double measure of Cointreau poured over for good measure. How about that?' And he plonked it down in front of her before tucking into his steaming treacle tart – with extra custard.

Alice looked at the melting sickly sweet vanilla ice cream, swimming in spirits, with a delight that only years of lessons in the niceties of social decorum could have made convincing.

And Edu looked so pleased with himself as he licked his plate clean.

Time for a siesta on the beach, with Elgar flat on his back snoring and Alice sitting bolt upright, dozing beneath the shade of her parasol – which, she imagined, declared her exalted status like a royal pennant flying proudly in the breeze.

She was simply an English lady of quality, modestly keeping up the standards and traditions of her class – as Queen Victoria would have been the first to acknowledge, had she happened to drive by while taking the afternoon air in the Royal Landau.

But Queen Victoria was sleeping off a heavy lunch miles away at Osborne House and was as oblivious to Alice's sense of duty as was the slightly sloshed musician slumbering blissfully by her side.

Lie down beside him in the sand? She would rather die.

THREE

Consummation

HAT DOES ONE do on the Isle of Wight on one's honeymoon? Stay in bed all day and make love perhaps. As things transpired, Elgar had no choice – Alice was unfortunately in 'a certain condition', so they were confined to sleep and sightseeing.

And as it happened they were spoiled for choice. Day excursions to Ryde and Cowes were followed by more adventurous activities, such as going for a paddle in Freshwater Bay – aptly named, according to Alice.

'Look, Edu, my tiny tootsies have turned quite blue with cold.'

This was followed by a search for fossils at Shanklin. Alice found a beauty, which poor Edu was lumbered with for the rest of the day.

Next there was a scramble down the cliffs at Alum Bay to scrape multi-coloured grains of sand into small glass containers in the shape of the lighthouse just along the coast at the Needles. That was fun, until Alice got a speck of sand in her eye.

The next day they bought postcards and wrote to relatives and friends during what turned out to be a mediocre concert in the Botanical Gardens – enlivened by the vigorous performance of two Scottish collies under their very noses.

'Quite appropriate, don't you think?' said Elgar, giving Alice a nudge.

Alice glanced up and then quickly averted her gaze. 'What do you mean, Edu?' she exclaimed disapprovingly.

'The music – "Sheep May Safely Graze",' he replied with a ripe guffaw.

Alice tut-tutted and, returning to her postcards, prayed that the deplorable spectacle would not give Edu any ideas.

On their next to last day Elgar and Alice decided to venture further afield and took a ferry to Lymington, a pretty town on the mainland. From there they caught a train to Brockenhurst in the New Forest, where Alice nearly trod on an adder.

'Don't worry, darling,' said Elgar. 'I'm almost sure it's a grass snake. They're harmless, you know.'

'I'm positive it's an adder snake,' persisted Alice, stabbing it expertly through the back of the head with a swift jab of her parasol. Elgar was shocked. Snakes held no fears for Alice, who had dealt with them since childhood during the days of the Raj in Rawalpindi.

However, it was their first serious disagreement, which cost Elgar half a bottle of champagne on the trip back on the ferry to Yarmouth.

'Sorry I don't have the right change, Edu,' sniffed Alice, buttressing her wounded pride with a posture of unyielding dignity. But lack of funds didn't stop her scouring the bookshops of that little seaside town for a book on local reptiles. And by the time she had found one and triumphantly proved her point with an emphatic recitation of the text, the couple had missed the last public conveyance back to Ventnor. That meant hiring a hansom cab at some considerable expense, which had Elgar silently fuming during the entire twenty-five-mile journey.

Matters were not improved when they arrived back to find the love nest in total darkness.

'Knock quietly,' said Alice. 'We don't want to wake everyone.'

An obvious retort sprang to mind, but Elgar bit his tongue, expressing his frustration by sounding such a rat-a-tat-tat as to awaken the entire terrace. Alice winced as he repeated the action again and again.

They'd missed supper, and the dining-room had already been set for breakfast, so they had to put up with cold meat and pickles, delivered to their room by a fuming landlady with her hair in curlers. Throughout the meal, which they choked down in silence, Alice tried to find words to tell Edu that she was no longer in purdah – unsuccessfully. She became distraught, but Elgar didn't notice.

So, if she had died of a broken heart on this penultimate night of the honeymoon, she would have died a virgin. With this sad thought uppermost in her mind she cried herself to sleep – silently, so as not to wake Edu.

But it hadn't been all doom and gloom by any means. Generally speaking, they got on well together and had a good time; particularly at Sandown, where seeing a child's cricket set in the window of a toy shop prompted Alice to mention that her elder brother – who was mad about the game – had taught her how to play. A short time later she was knocking Elgar's bowling into the briny, as a gang of willing kids acted as enthusiastic fielders.

Eventually, Alice twisted her wrist in bowling Elgar a googly, whereupon the adults bequeathed the set to the youngsters and retired to tea. Despite the minor injury, that was probably the highlight of their stay.

On their last day it rained, which did little to raise their spirits, dampened by the events of the previous day. So they went their separate ways. Elgar ventured forth to brave the elements. Alice opted to stay indoors and take a stab at what she liked best – daydreaming and turning her flights of fancy into poetry.

Elgar was also daydreaming, in a deserted public shelter facing out to sea on the front. What had started off as light drizzle had developed into a heavy downpour. So Elgar decided to sit out the storm and think of music.

But uppermost in his mind was his falling out with Alice. Had he made a big mistake? Was the marriage doomed to failure? If only he had wedded his dream girl – if only. And as he idly contemplated the wind-swept waters his mind returned unbidden to the moment he had thrown that bottle in the direction of New Zealand, leading him to wonder how it might be progressing.

There was a message in that bottle – written on a single sheet of manuscript. It was a piano piece composed by Elgar and jotted down in his own firm hand. The music had a title, La Blonde. In its original version it had been scored for the staff band that performed for the inmates at the Worcestershire County Lunatic Asylum at Powick. Elgar was the visiting bandmaster, for which he was paid thirty-two pounds per annum, plus an additional fee for every dance tune. For La Blonde, a lively polka, he received the sum of five pounds, which he spent in treating the smashing blonde in question to a slap-up meal.

Her name was Helen Weaver, and if anyone could claim to be his very first sweetheart it was she. Friends since childhood, they had remained constant companions in their teens, and by the time they had reached their mid-twenties were engaged to be married ... until she suddenly broke it off and sailed away to New Zealand.

Elgar was devastated. His friends despaired of him, as they debated the possible reasons for her sudden departure. Was it on religious grounds – they held incompatible beliefs – or was it for reasons of health? Helen had tuber-culosis, and in the annals of medical history no sufferer had ever been sent to

England for a cure. The friends continued to wonder, but Elgar refused to pander to their curiosity. It was too personal, too painful.

The rain had stopped. Should he wander back and make the peace over lunch? Or should he have a bite in the pub across the road? He still had a little pocket money left.

The pub won the contest. It was a change to be off duty, so to speak, and surely he should make the most of it. Besides, there was the ghost of a theme beginning to haunt the recesses of his mind, and who knows? A few pints followed by a brisk walk along the beach, rain or no rain, might entice it into the open.

By the time he got back, damp but not downhearted, it was dark and the room was empty. He lit the oil lamp and noticed a couple of notes on the writing desk. He picked one up and read it out loud.

'In the upstairs bathroom, Edu, enjoying a good soak after being hunched over a writing desk all day.' He wouldn't mind a hot bath himself, come to think of it, and wondered if the bathroom on the ground floor might be free.

The other piece of paper contained a short poem – efforts of much labour, if the crammed waste-paper basket was anything to go by. It read:

> Closely let me hold thy hand
> Storms are sweeping sea and land
> Love alone will stand
> Closely cling, for waves beat fast
> Foam-flakes cloud the hurrying blast
> Love alone will last
> Kiss my lips and softly say:
> Joy, sea-swept, may fade today
> Love alone will stay

Elgar wondered if he were dreaming. The phantom melody he had been struggling with all day had suddenly materialized, fully formed as the perfect accompaniment to Alice's verse. It was uncanny. The word 'synchronicity' was not in Elgar's vocabulary, but 'eureka' certainly was, and that is what he cried out before running up the stairs and along the landing to the bathroom door, fairly shaking with excitement.

'Listen to this, darling! Bless you!' he shouted at the top of his voice.

That word 'darling' again – it must have been heard all over the house. Thank God they couldn't see her blushes and that she'd wedged a chair firmly beneath the doorknob. Had the man taken leave of his senses?

She was soon to find out, as in a fine tenor voice Elgar started to broadcast their song to the world. Whereupon Alice's despair immediately gave way to a cry of joy, as the realization of their extraordinary achievement finally hit home.

That night their marriage was consummated.

FOUR

When Knights Were Bold

AFTER THE HONEYMOON, they bounced between Malvern and the Metropolis for a while, before taking a three-year lease on a small terraced house in West Kensington – the unfashionable side of the Royal Borough. It was dark and gloomy and all they could afford on Alice's ever-shrinking nest-egg.

But they were determined to make the best of it, their main objective being to establish Elgar as an up-and-coming composer – one to be reckoned with. With the help of a housemaid and cook Alice entertained visiting dignitaries from the West Country who, if not dazzled by Elgar's prospects, were at least reassured by the high polish on her inherited silver. Her obvious loyalty to the social code of her birth and her offering of high tea and high-society chit-chat made it easier for them to consider him 'interesting' – if not exactly the budding genius extolled by Alice.

Meanwhile, the questionable genius was tramping the streets of Soho, rain and muck up to his spats, his worn boots just one more bloody social embarrassment he'd be damned if he'd admit to, trying to interest publishers in a variety of brief salon pieces. Here was Liebesgruss, for instance, which he had originally written for Alice as an engagement present.

'Uh . . . Excuse me, what did you say?'

'Your Liebesgruss, Mr Elgar,' the man from Schott's Publishers was saying. 'We'll want to change the title, of course. It's standard procedure. And if you agree, we're prepared to offer you five pounds for the publishing rights, without further discussion.'

Call it what you like, thought Elgar, if it means you'll buy it! What do I care? It's my music people will remember, not the bloody title!

So Schott's paid Elgar five pounds for the world rights, subsequently changed the title to Salut d'Amour and made a fortune. With the proceeds Elgar treated Alice to the famous Crystal Palace at Upper Norwood for its London première.

She was entranced and rightly so. Salut d'Amour is a love song without words if ever there was one. Its haunting melodies are imbued with a seductive nostalgia for long summer days shared with a dear companion, promising an eternity of bliss. Or so Alice thought when Edu first played it to her on the piano.

Now, hearing it performed just for her by a full symphony orchestra, here in this Palace of Crystal, she was in seventh heaven. The fact that there were two thousand eavesdroppers didn't concern her in the least. Indeed, she was quite thrilled by the fact, because they had all read their programme notes and knew the romantic origins of the piece. And when Elgar rose to take a bow at the behest of the conductor, they all knew that the proud lady at his side had inspired the exquisite miniature receiving such rapturous applause. The event was a real turn-on. Alice could hardly wait to get back to their bedroom and get down on her hands and knees.

Yes, the day had finally dawned when Alice had succumbed to the inevitable and, contrary to her expectation regarding a 'wife's duty', suffered the experience gladly. It was another way she could prove her love for her 'Edu'; though – try as she may – she could never quite erase the memory of those two romping collie dogs from her mind.

Some months previously Elgar had received a commission to compose an orchestral work for the Three Choirs Festival. These were annual music extravaganzas held in the adjacent Cathedrals of Hereford, Gloucester and Worcester, each of which took it in turn to try and outdo the others in performance and excellence. This year the event was to be hosted by his home town of Worcester. And, though Elgar had turned his back on it to seek fame and fortune in London, there were obviously no hard feelings.

For his part, Elgar was truly grateful, especially as the Metropolis had steadfastly failed to welcome him with open arms. Yes, he'd sold a few pieces that had provided a little pocket money, but as yet he had not been offered one solitary commission.

Then early one morning a letter from the Festival Committee asking him for a progress report finally spurred him into action – this, together with the news that Alice was pregnant. Soon there would be another mouth to feed.

Elgar secretly named the coming usurper 'the Cuckoo', for – regardless of its sex – its arrival would undoubtedly presage the swift disposal of their much-coveted nest-egg.

In the study after breakfast he sat at his desk, looking at the blank manuscript before him. His mind, too, was blank. He looked out of the window, veiled in lace curtains. The outside world of bricks and mortar was an uninspiring abstraction. He dipped his pen into an inkwell, hoping this promising start would fool his brain into producing results.

Nothing! He closed his eyes, partly because they were giving him trouble, partly to shut out the suffocating vision of domesticity he saw drawing ever closer about him. But he could not shut out the aural world filtering in from the street – the occasional snatches of conversation from passers-by and the incessant clip-clop of horses' hooves that dominated everything.

Elgar's irritation at finding himself in a pitched battle with an inspiration that eluded him slowly began to subside in spite of himself. Noble creatures, he thought. That's what horses are. Noble creatures. There was a time when man, too, had been noble. The chronicles of Froissart was one of the most well-thumbed volumes on his bookshelf. Those were days, eh? When chivalry raised her lance on high!

Thoughts of knights and damsels in distress inevitably led to thoughts of his first love – his lost love – and a memorable fancy-dress summer fête in Malvern where they had won first prize as 'the perfect couple'. And there had been plenty of rival contestants for the judges to consider, from half a dozen Romeos and Juliets to a motley collection of Robin Hoods and Maid Marians. But the verdict was unanimous . . .

'And the winners are . . . Miss Helen Weaver and Mr Edward Elgar, as the fair Lady Guinevere and bold Sir Lancelot.'

General applause followed as the knight and his damsel mounted the platform to receive two Staffordshire figures, a shepherd and shepherdess, as the band played a flourish of 'Rule Britannia'.

Elgar opened his eyes and looked towards the chimney-piece where, next to the clock with reclining figure, stood the much-prized shepherdess. Elgar had gone apoplectic when Alice had broken the news that Sarah was guilty of a slight dusting misdemeanour. And when he rushed into the backyard, emptied the dustbin and sorted through the contents, in his best clothes, the dear lady thought he had taken leave of his senses – and so did the servants. Such a fuss over such a nondescript ornament. It wasn't even genuine Royal Dalton, just a cheap copy.

Fortunately, it had broken into just three pieces, and from where Elgar was now sitting at his desk the figure he had so lovingly restored looked as good as new.

'It has great sentimental value,' said Elgar in clipped tones, by way of an explanation for his outburst. Alice kept to herself her observation that it was out of all proportion to the article's intrinsic value. As for poor Sarah, she considered herself lucky to have escaped with her life and trembled anew whenever it was time to dust it.

Elgar was also trembling, for quite another reason. In fact, he was close to tears, remembering that moment when they had stood together on that platform, hand in hand, she in ribbons and silks and he in borrowed armour, before an admiring crowd of well-wishers, cheering them to the echo.

Alas, that was an age long past, when the future promised him a noble quest for the holy grail of music, with his devoted lady at his side. Was there to be nothing now but chasing fools' errands, scrabbling in dustbins after broken pieces, for men who once dared to dream?

But even the memory of that dream still meant something – something compelling enough to turn his creative spark into a glow, which at once began to fire his imagination. Inspired, he dipped his pen into the ink again and commenced to attack the manuscript before him with heroic vigour.

And if Alice played no part in the concept of the Concert Overture Froissart, to give the new work its official title, she certainly helped in a practical way – by ruling the bar lines on his scores. She took great satisfaction in knowing she could save him time and secure his environment for composition alone. It kept her from thinking about her condition – something she hoped wouldn't interfere with the bliss of her twosome with Elgar.

And only two months after Elgar had first put pen to paper the finished work had been accepted by Novello's and was already at the printers. For the very first time the players would have properly engraved parts for an Elgar première.

Then, just as preparations for the big event were under way, Elgar was upstaged by another event – the arrival of the cuckoo in the nest. Yes, on 14 August 1890 Caroline Alice gave birth to a baby daughter that Elgar nicknamed 'the Anagram', on the occasion of her being christened Carice. Both parents were as proud as peacocks, with Elgar dangling the little fledgling on his knee – until an unfortunate accident, after which he cheerfully changed her nickname to 'the Peahen'.

Even so, the joyous event brought a tinge of sadness with it, when the nursing mother was forced to miss the première of Edu's first big orchestral work. 'I shall be there in spirit, dear Edu,' she said, as she kissed her knight in shining armour goodbye at the front door of their Englishperson's castle.

The next day Alice bought every London daily paper and scanned every column to locate the name she was sure had just made history. But the only mention of Elgar was in the 'Situations Vacant' column of *The Times*, which had cost her a postal order for £3 13s. It read:

> Experienced professional violin teacher
> ex-member of Worcester Festival orch.
> available for private tuition for limited
> number of gifted pupils in central London area.
> (Reply Box No. E 711)

It had been running for a week, and this was the last day – and so far not a single reply.

Her extreme disappointment was alleviated somewhat when her doughty knight returned from his quest for fame, brandishing a copy of the *Worcester Daily News*. But on reading the headline at the head of the review her gloom returned: 'Shopkeeper's Son Throws Down Gauntlet to Musical Knights of Low Endeavour'.

'I hope you haven't shown this to anyone yet, Edu,' exclaimed Alice, before biting her tongue.

'What do you mean?' demanded Elgar. 'It's wonderful! It compares me favourably to all the established Sir Goddamn Awfuls and Lord Pompous Asses. Read it! Read it!'

Alice did so. The review, written by a close friend of Elgar, sang his praises, true enough; but to Alice the article was primarily a stick for beating the teachers and graduates of the conservative music academies – with which Elgar had never been associated. An awkward silence ensued.

'Shall we dress for dinner, Edu?' said Alice, by way of changing the subject.

'I had something on the train,' sniffed Elgar, hurt by her evasion. 'Any reply to the ad?'

Alice's forced enthusiasm was a little too transparent. 'Not so far, Edu, but there's still time.'

'Sheer waste of money,' said Elgar, smouldering. 'Just as I predicted.'

Another awkward silence, broken by the distant yell of the little Peahen.

'I must go to Carice,' insisted Alice, grateful for a means of escape. 'She's hungry.'

'Yes. Go stick your flat old tit in her mouth; shut her up, for once! All she does is yell, yell, yell; morning, noon and night . . . I'm going where I can hear myself think!'

And as Alice hurried upstairs feeling totally wretched she winced as she heard the front door slam. Elgar was off to drown his sorrows.

FIVE

Wandering Lonely as a Cloud

*T*HE CRISIS OF domestic quarrel soon passed, to be replaced by brittle anxiety. Elgar started going to church again, breaking the pattern of truancy he had established during his total commitment to composing Froissart. He was driven less by an impulse to atone than by a desperate hunger for a little peace and quiet.

What next? The thought obsessed him even while on his knees during the service. He considered writing a violin concerto but lacked inspiration. He tried conjuring up a muse in the shape of Helen Weaver, but – for the moment at least – it seemed that she had abandoned him.

He was lost in a fog, both spiritually and physically. He went from clouds of incense in the church to pea-soupers in the streets, so penetrating that they even stole under the doors and haunted every room in the house, spooking the inhabitants. Sarah had the snivels, Cook limped with rheumatism, Alice shivered with cold no matter how many fires were lit, and Elgar complained of headaches and sore eyes. Carice alone seemed unaffected and if sheer noise were anything to go by, had the healthiest pair of lungs in the house.

To make matters worse, the nest-egg was only a memory. Alice had to sell her exquisite pearl choker. Her practical side insisted on the sacrifice, but she secretly found herself imagining ghostly reprisals from the line of stern, well-dressed women who had worn it before her.

Elgar, having advertised unsuccessfully in London for pupils, was forced to renew contact with the Mount, the ladies' college in Malvern where, in less taxing times, he had frequently given classes in the violin. He tried to keep the phrase 'crawling back, hat in hand' out of his mental repertoire as he offered them his services. He needn't have worried. They were only too happy to take him back. Now Elgar could add to his burdens a constant round of tiring train journeys with extensive stopovers.

Seeing her beleaguered genius grow more drawn and numb with each prolonged commute, Alice was not slow to realize that the game was hardly worth the candle. Elgar's forced marches had not put the wolf at the door off the scent. And with the aid of a skinful of Dutch courage she determined to tell Elgar so one damp November night.

He had arrived home worn and weary in the middle of a putrid pea-souper that had been laying about for several days and was almost as thick as the real thing but less nourishing. In fact, it was lethal. As they sat in front of a roaring fire after a hearty meal, Alice wondered how best to introduce the subject.

Perhaps she should try the direct approach?

We're financially embarrassed, Edu. We can no longer afford to live in London, so let's cut our losses and go back home.

But that implied defeat and would surely shatter Edu's confidence – what was left of it. Besides, this was their home. The family seat at Redmarley was miles away from Malvern and would soon be up for sale in order to top up their meagre income. She would have to find another excuse, one that he could not possibly object to, one that would not dent his pride.

She picked on Peahen – Carice.

'The poor little thing has weak lungs, Edu, dear,' she said, stretching credibility. 'I called the doctor to examine her while you were away; and he feared for her survival should she remain here, at the mercy of this appalling weather. Edu, we must leave London for your daughter's sake.'

It was a request Elgar was powerless to refuse, even if he had wanted to.

'Very well, old girl,' he replied. 'Carice's health is of prime importance. I would rather bury my hopes than bury our child. Let's put the lease of the house up for sale tomorrow. The sooner we get out of this Godforsaken place the better.'

In less than a month they were on the train to Malvern, whence, despite putting a bold face on it, Elgar was returning a chastened man with a heavy heart.

SIX

The New Woman

'**G**OOD MORNING, I believe Mr Elgar is expecting me,' said an attractive young woman to Sarah the maid, when she answered the door one damp summer's day in response to an impatient tattoo. Sarah noticed with alarm that the woman was holding one of those new-fangled machines that were threatening the lives of God-fearing pedestrians such as herself.

'Who shall I say is calling, madam?' she asked, looking askance at the visitor's outlandish garb.

'My name is Rosa Burley, and please may I come in out of the rain?'

Sarah hesitated. This must be one of those new women she'd heard tell of, the kind who chained themselves to railings and blew up pillar-boxes.

'I'd like to bring my bicycle into the hallway, if you don't mind,' she said, brushing past her.

'You can wait in the drawing-room,' said the intimidated Sarah, indicating an open door. 'I'll see if the master is at home.'

And as Miss Burley gave a little snigger and entered the front room with its big bay windows Sarah made off to face the master's wrath. She had never let a stranger into the house unannounced before, and she feared his reaction – he'd been awfully short of late.

Meanwhile Miss Burley amused herself by taking a mental inventory of the bizarre furnishings surrounding her, many of which would not have been out of place in the home of an Indian raja. Footsteps on the stairs caused her to wipe the smile off her face and look serious.

When Elgar entered the room, her demeanour changed yet again, but this time her reaction was both unpremeditated and unexpected. In fact, she gasped with surprise – and admiration. Standing before her was the most striking man she had ever seen.

Elgar, too, had caught his breath. The love of his life, Helen Weaver, had returned to him and was standing there in the person of this woman who stared open-mouthed.

'Snap,' said Elgar, once he had recovered his composure.

'Snap,' replied Miss Burley, on getting the connection. From the waist down they were both garbed in a similar fashion – he in plus-fours tucked into knee-length stockings, she in bloomers tucked into knee-length stockings – both revealing a shapely leg and a trim ankle. She did bear a superficial resemblance to Helen, it is true, but more elfin and with something of the tomboy about her, no doubt exaggerated by her clothes. They sized each other up in silence, and the longer the silence lasted the more difficult it became to break, for, truth to tell, it was lust at first sight.

Who could have predicted it, even a minute ago? When Sarah had burst into his study and blurted out that there was an odd-looking woman with a bicycle waiting for him downstairs Elgar was furious at the intrusion and had decided to give his impertinent visitor a frosty reception. But the moment he set eyes on her he melted.

'Excuse me for staring,' Elgar finally managed to get out, 'but I was expecting a headmistress in a more conventional mode of dress.'

'What, a mortar and gown, you mean?' said Miss Burley with a wicked grin.

'No, not quite that,' laughed Elgar, admiring her rakish, oversized school-boy cap and checked blouse, 'but, you know, something a little more prim and proper perhaps.'

'Well, you're not exactly the traditional picture of a composer yourself, are you? I was expecting someone in a smock and floppy hat, rather like Wagner. You look more like a country gentleman ready for a little huntin', fishin' and shootin'!'

'Actually, I'm just off for a round of golf with Hughie Blair. Do you know him?'

'I'm afraid not.'

'Just taken over from old Will Done or old "Well Done" as we used to call him – resident organist down at the Cathedral.'

'I'm new to the district. I know no one,' she confessed. 'You must introduce me.'

'Pleasure. You'll like him. You have something in common.'

'Music, you mean?'

'That, too, but I mean the bicycle – pedals all over the place. Gloucester, Hereford, even as far as Birmingham.'

'Well, that makes two of us.'

'Good Lord,' said Elgar in admiration, then, as an afterthought, 'You were chaperoned, of course?'

At this Miss Burley laughed. 'On the contrary, I was chaperoning a class of schoolgirls. Do you have a bicycle, Mr Elgar?'

'Heavens, no,' exclaimed Elgar. 'I leave that sort of thing to clowns at the circus.' Then, feeling his visitor might be insulted, added, 'Besides, I'd never keep my balance.'

'It's easy once you get the hang of it. I'd be happy to give you lessons.'

Before Elgar could reply the door burst open and Alice swept in. She had been listening at the keyhole and decided the moment had come to break up the tête-à-tête, as she was far from happy with the way it was going.

'Alice, this is Miss Burley, the new headmistress at the Mount. Miss Burley, this is my wife Alice.'

'How do you do,' said Alice.

'How do you do,' replied Miss Burley. 'Your husband and I were discussing the possibility of him giving lessons at the Mount.'

'He has been teaching at the Mount for some considerable time.'

'Only on a part-time basis, I believe. I'd like to propose a more regular involvement.'

Alice balked at the word 'involvement', for she was no fool and and was quite aware of their mutual attraction.

'I doubt that Edward could spare the time, Miss Burley,' said Alice. 'It would interfere with his work as a full-time composer.'

'Oh, I am sorry, Mr Elgar. Do tell me, what are you working on just now?'

For a second Elgar was stymied. He resented Alice's interference but also appreciated her concern for his work – only now did it occur to him that she might be jealous.

'Well, to be perfectly frank, I'm working on nothing at this precise moment; so, yes, I would certainly like to consider the possibility.'

'Excellent,' said Miss Burley. 'Perhaps you'd like to come down to the school to discuss matters further.'

'Splendid. Splendid.'

'Shall we say Thursday at eleven?' asked Miss Burley, making for the hall, sensing correctly that, as far as Alice was concerned, she was outstaying her welcome. 'At the same time I can show you a bicycle catalogue, if you are interested.'

'Very much so,' said Elgar, opening the front door for her.

'My pleasure.'

'Goodbye, Miss Burley,' said Alice coldly.

'Goodbye, Mrs Elgar.'

'So, till eleven o'clock on Thursday, then, Miss Burley,' called Elgar after her.

'Oh, do call me Rosa,' she laughed over her shoulder, wheeling her bike to the gate.

'Goodbye, Rosa,' said Elgar, laughing in return.

Alice, however, was not amused.

Husband and wife watched Rosa intently as she cycled, no hands, down the road and around the corner.

'My Lord,' said Elgar, 'did you see that, darling? No hands!'

'No brains either,' muttered Alice as she stomped off to see Cook.

'Goodbye, darling,' shouted Elgar as he grabbed his hat and golf bag from the hall stand. He didn't wait for a reply, which in the circumstances was just as well.

When he returned at dusk, he noticed that the drawing-room was bathed in the glow of a paraffin lamp. Surreptitiously he peered through the window and wondered what a curious passer-by would have made of the spectacle of a smartly dressed middle-aged lady sitting on a sandalwood throne surrounded by relics of the Raj, including two obscure Hindu gods, a gong, a tiger-skin rug, an oil painting of the Major-General, a knob kerrie, a pair of tusks and a bust of Queen Victoria.

But what caught his eye was a basket full of books on the table that Alice was in the process of studying. This he took as a good sign, in so far as she obviously was not brooding over Miss Burley.

'Is that you, Edu?' she asked, on hearing him dump his golf bag in the hall.

'Yes, precious,' he replied, entering the drawing-room and kissing her on the forehead. Trying her best not to react to his boozy breath, Alice smiled up at him.

'Did you have a good round?'

'Not until we got to the nineteenth, darling, and then I really made up for it,' he guffawed. 'But it wasn't a totally wasted afternoon. Hughie Blair has promised to produce my next orchestral work in Worcester.'

'Oh, Edu, what wonderful news. I must be psychic.'

'Good heavens! Does that mean you're going to tell my fortune?'

'Not at all, Edu. But I can certainly help you make one.'

'Exactly how, O Psychic Guide?' he asked incredulously.

'By guiding you in the right direction, my dear.'

'Speak on, fair soothsayer. I'm all ears.'

'All the better to hear me with,' Alice replied, little realizing she would live to regret this slip into the world of fairy-tale.

'So, tell me,' said Elgar, glad of the chance to delay the oracle's dictum, 'what sweet treats has Little Red Riding Hood brought Granny in her basket today?'

Alice, following his glance to the basket brimming with books, deemed it expedient to play along. 'Food for thought, O Granny, dear. I've been to the library.'

'Granny's hungry, all right, but not for library books,' growled Elgar.

'Then tell me, Granny, dear,' replied Alice in childlike tones, 'what would you have instead?'

'I'd have you, my dear,' roared Elgar.

'Oh, please, Mr Wolf, spare me, spare me!'

This was greeted by a howl that would have done credit to a werewolf.

Oh, what have I started? fretted Alice to herself; not for the first time, as she watched Elgar lock the door and blow out the oil lamp. And in less time than it takes to tell Little Red Riding Hood was on her hands and knees with her dress flung over her head, being ravaged by a voracious wolf. This was something she had not prophesied, but at least he wouldn't be thinking of Rosa Burley.

Or would he?

SEVEN

Bon Mots

COME THURSDAY MORNING Alice was in the drawing-room studying her library books when she heard the front door slam. For the first time Elgar had left the house without kissing her goodbye. Impulsively she jumped to her feet and knocked loudly on the window. Elgar, on his way to the gate, almost jumped out of his skin as he spun around to see her, his face a picture of guilt. For a moment they stared at each other – blankly – until Elgar pulled himself together, shrugged off his forgetfulness, smiled and blew her a kiss.

Alice responded in like manner, after which they both waved goodbye, and that was that. Well, not quite that, because the incident had raised a doubt in Alice's mind – a doubt she would rather not dwell on. So she returned to her self-imposed task of sifting through reams of nineteenth-century verse.

The Mount boarding-school had always put Elgar in mind of a vast nunnery, row after row of Gothic windows five stories high surmounted by a steep church-like roof. And if the teenage girls weren't exactly dressed as nuns, their long black skirts and blouses of virgin white helped towards creating the hushed ecclesiastical atmosphere that invariably enveloped Elgar whenever he entered the building.

And this particular Thursday was no exception, until he entered the office of the new headmistress Rosa Burley. The religious overtones favoured by the previous incumbent had been subtly transformed into something vaguely decadent and disturbing. Elgar's appreciation of high art stopped with the Pre-Raphaelites; names such as Whistler and Aubrey Beardsley were unknown to him. And it was the latter that Rosa had taken as her inspiration for both costume and décor – for everything was in black and white in a sort of mockery of the religious orders.

'Still dressed for golf, I see,' said Rosa after the introductions were over and they were seated. 'Are you off for another round? I wonder you get any work done.'

'No, these are my working clothes, Miss Rosa. I, too, have my unconventional side. I save my suit for Sunday mass.'

'Do you think my bum looks big in bloomers?' asked Rosa, standing up and twirling around.

For the first time in years Elgar was speechless.

'You look as if you've just seen a ghost,' said Alice to her husband, when he arrived home two hours later.

No, not a ghost, but a lady of spirit, thought Elgar, as he searched for a suitable reply.

'Come in, you must be weak from hunger. It's way past your lunchtime,' said his wife.

'I could eat a horse, darling,' he said, wiping his feet on the doormat.

'Oh dear, I'm afraid you'll have to make do with Bœuf Wellington, Edu. Can you bear it?'

'Well, if it was good enough for the Iron Duke I'm sure it is good enough for me . . . Such a chatterbox, that woman,' he added, rushing upstairs to wash his hands. 'But in the circumstances, it was well worth putting up with.'

'Really,' Alice shouted after him, sweeping off to organize the kitchen.

'Tell you all about it over lunch,' Elgar shouted back.

'Bœuf Wellington, eh,' said Elgar on tucking into a brimming plate a few minutes later. 'His favourite dish, you say? No wonder he had the strength to boot Old Boney out of Waterloo.'

'And so much more succulent than "roast beef in a case of pastry", don't you agree, Edu?'

'Shorter, too,' replied Elgar, smacking his lips.

'Edu, do forgive me, but,' – she nodded towards him – 'a little gravy, there on your moustache.'

Momentarily taken aback, Elgar made light of it. 'I'm saving it for seconds,' he laughed. 'Waste not, want not.'

'Oh, do use your napkin, please, Edu,' said Alice discreetly. 'It's congealing and looks like . . .'

'Like what?' said Elgar testily.

'Like . . .' Alice hesitated.

'Say it,' said Elgar brusquely. 'Snot. Honest-to-goodness snot. Nothing to be ashamed of, snot.'

Another pause.

'I was going to say mucus, darling,' Alice said in strangled tones, falling into his habit of speech.

Elgar was furious. 'Mucus, Bœuf Wellington, Gratin Dauphinoise, Sorbet, Steak au Poivre – whatever happened to good old peppered steak? And what's this napkin business. If you mean "serviette" say serviette,' and he tore his 'serviette' from his collar, threw it down on his plate and stormed out of the room, shouting, 'And don't bother to wait. I won't be back for afters.'

Alice dropped her head and gave way to tears, as Edu's discarded napkin began to soak up the rich wine gravy. The gravy on her own plate was becoming more salty by the minute and more diluted with it. A light tap on the door announced Sarah, who cleared everything away without a word – until she was about to leave the room with her tray.

'Will Madam be taking dessert today?' she asked quietly.

Had she emphasized the word 'dessert'? Alice wondered. Sarah, too, had insisted on calling desserts 'sweets' and 'afters' just like Edu but had proved a more apt pupil by far.

'No, neither of us will be taking dessert today. You may serve coffee in the drawing-room in fifteen minutes' time.'

'Will that be coffee for one, madam?' said Sarah, still hovering.

Alice hesitated only a moment. 'Two,' she announced emphatically. 'And remind Mr Edward to join me, will you?'

'Very well, madam,' said Sarah, closing the door awkwardly behind her and fairly dreading the task before her.

Twenty minutes later Alice entered the drawing-room to find Elgar with his back towards her, arms folded, ostensibly staring out of the window. He remained motionless, wondering if Alice had forgiven his unwarranted outburst.

'You were going to tell me about your encounter with the eccentric Miss Burley,' said Alice, approaching the coffee tray. 'May I pour for you, Edu?'

'Er, yes, thank you,' said Elgar, reassured by her equanimity. 'Black for me, please, darling, with just a *soupçon* of brandy, if I may.'

Alice almost raised an eyebrow at Edu's first foray into the French of common usage but managed to restrain the impulse.

And as Alice did the honours and handed him a cup of fortified coffee Elgar surprised her further by saying, 'Thank you, *ma petite choux*.'

'*Mon,*' said Alice after a pause.

'More?' responded Elgar, genuinely perplexed.

'You said *ma*. *Ma*,' insisted Alice, unable to control her instinct for correction.

'I said *Mama*?'

'It's *mon petit choux* – cabbage is masculine.'

But this was too much for Elgar, even trying his utmost to be on his best behaviour. 'How the hell can a cabbage be masculine? Does a cabbage have a cock, for Chrissakes?'

Alice left the room.

Good God, he'd made yet another balls-up – after searching all over the study for the French–English/English–French dictionary of useful words and phrases, feverishly searching its pages in a wild hope of making amends. Blast it! Now what?

He was still wondering, when he happened to notice an open book lying on the table. He glanced at it, glanced again and picked it up. It was a poetry anthology. 'The Black Knight' was the title that first met his eye. Above it was the word 'Edu' written in pencil. Intrigued, Elgar started to read:

> 'Twas Pentecost, the feast of gladness
> When woods and fields put off all sadness
> Thus began the King and spoke:
> 'So from the Hall of ancient Hofburg's walls
> A luxuriant spring shall break.'

Hooked, he read on and on, engrossed in a Gothic tale about death in the form of a mysterious knight encased in sinister black armour, who attends the feast in order to claim two of the King's innocent children.

The last verse particularly grabbed him:

> Woe the blessed children both
> Takest thou in the joy of youth;

Take me, too, the joyless father!
Spoke the grim guest,
From his hollow, cavernous breast;
'Roses in the Spring I gather!'

Only then did Elgar become aware of Alice standing in the doorway. He barely had time to register her presence before she broke the silence.

'It's a translation from the German. The original is by Johann Ludwig Uhland.'

'Never heard of him,' said Elgar gruffly, still feeling aggrieved.

'Well, what do you think?'

'Good old Gothic claptrap,' said Elgar, somewhat more amiably. 'Is that all you think I'm fit for, setting third-rate Kraut verse to music? I presume that is the reason you drew it to my attention.'

'It's perfect material for an oratorio, Edu,' said Alice, entering the room and confronting him.

'Oratorio,' he said, raising his eyes to heaven, 'the millstone around the neck of English music.'

'You must learn to give the public what it wants, Edu; and it wants oratorios.'

'Every third-rate composer in the country is churning out oratorios. There's a glut of them.'

'Perhaps, but they certainly put Sir Hubert Parry on the map.'

'Oh, rest ye in the Lord! He'd set the whole damn Bible to music given half a chance.'

'Well, at least "The Black Knight" isn't a religious piece.'

'I've already chosen a subject for a new work, anyway,' he told her with a certain amount of apprehension.

'Since walking out of the house this morning?' said Alice, quite aghast. 'That's rather sudden, isn't it? You've been completely at a loss for months. Where did this sudden inspiration come from? Don't tell me, I can guess.'

Another silence was followed by a sheepish response. 'Well, if you must know, I was discussing my future career with Miss Burley, and . . .' Here he hesitated.

'Were you indeed?' said Alice indignantly. 'And why not consult the cook while you're at it?'

'Miss Burley is well versed in my music. She wants me to teach her young ladies my "Serenade for Strings".'

'Mass murder. Well, go on, tell me, what did she suggest for a new composition: concerto for bicycle-pump and orchestra with herself as soloist?'

At this Elgar gave an involuntary chuckle, which somehow broke the ice – whereupon he flopped down on to an armchair, pulling Alice gently on to his lap. He put his arm around her waist and kissed her on the lips. Alice did not resist, but she did not respond either.

'Sorry, old girl,' he said. 'The headaches have come back. Makes me a bit grumpy.'

'Is it a secret, or do you want us to play a guessing game?'

'Of course not, darling. I have no secrets from you. You know that,' he told her reassuringly. 'If you must know, she suggested "The Charge of the Light Brigade".'

Alice gave a hoot, shot to her feet and paced about the room. 'What? That piece of doggerel, with the tenors booming "Cannons to the left of them" and the basses booming "Cannons to the right of them", and the sopranos shrieking "Volleyed and thundered". The idea is completely ludicrous.'

'Who said anything about an oratorio? Miss Burley suggested a symphonic poem.'

'Ha! Too late,' pronounced Alice triumphantly, determined to rubbish her rival. 'Tchaikovsky's beaten you to it. You've heard his "1812" Overture. In fact, we heard it together – in that all-Russian programme at the Crystal Palace. Remember?'

'I remember the cannon fire shattering several panes of glass,' said Elgar ruefully. 'Risky business, that.'

'And do you remember,' said Alice, now in her stride, 'remarking, as we brushed the glass from our laps, that the programme note should be amended to Tchaikovsky's "1812 Overture for Orchestra, Bells, Cannons and Casualties"?'

'I thought you said that,' chuckled Elgar.

'No, it was you, Edu. Or was it? I really can't remember. But don't you see, my love? It is simply out of the question. The critics would carve you up. "Who does he think he is, this little upstart from Worcester, daring to tread in the footsteps of the mighty Russian Master?" Not even the spectacle of Florence Nightingale in person being fired from a cannon could avert such a disastrous comparison, believe me!'

Alice was getting really heated by now, and when she flopped down on

Elgar's lap again she was flushed and breathy and her eyes were sparkling. She was that sweet-sixteen girl again.

This unaccustomed passion quite moved Elgar, in more ways than one, even though he was still unpersuaded. 'But if I do write an oratorio, I'll be compared with Parry and all the rest of them. It seems that either way I can't win.'

'But you can win,' said Alice fervently. 'With my favour fluttering on your lance you will unseat them at the lists and become the champion of the tournament, and "The Black Knight" will triumph in every choral event throughout the land. Do you know how many choral societies there are in the land, Edu?'

Elgar, hugely impressed, considered for a moment. 'There must be at least fifty, perhaps as many as seventy.'

'There are three hundred and thirteen,' said Alice solemnly. 'What do you think?'

'I think I've just found a new lucky number,' he said, kissing her tenderly. And this time she did respond.

EIGHT

Carice Speaks Out

And so a pattern was set that continued until the end of the century. Elgar continued to teach and supplement Alice's modest income. She, in turn, collaborated with him whenever possible, supplying words to his music, including songs from the Bavarian Highlands – inspired by holidays funded by generous friends in and around Garmish, a picturesque village just south of Munich.

Meanwhile the oratorios continued to appear with deadening regularity. In fact, it was a treadmill only made bearable by the support of friends of both sexes, including the invisible child, Carice.

Well, almost invisible, for like most children of her generation she was generally 'seen but not heard'. A holiday assignment for her headmistress inadvertently gives us a brief glimpse into life at Forli during the last decade of the century.

LIFE WITH FATHER BY CARICE ELGAR

I have never called Papa Father. This title I was given by my teacher, Miss Burley.

Papa calls me peahen. I don't know why. He calls me his little caddy too. I used to think a caddy was something you put tea in, now I know it's someone who carries a bag of golf clubs. They are heavy. Papa says it will make me strong.

Sometimes we go for walks. Papa likes walks. Mama likes walks too but is too busy to go with us. When Papa goes for walks with lady friends I stay behind. 2's company, 3's none he says.

When we go fishing I carry the net. I use it to catch butterflies. We never catch fish. You can't catch fish if you're asleep. Papa says he's thinking. But how can you think when you are snoring? That would be dreaming. I don't care for fishing much.

My best thing is when we go flying our kite up the hill when it's windy. That's exciting. It makes Papa happy. And I am happy too. We are both happy. That's where he finds his music. It's in the wind. All you have to do is catch it. I know that sounds easy but it's not. Why? Because it can catch you out. How? By blowing the other way, that's how. It's a tiring business is music, especially having to write it down. It seems to give you a headache and bad eyes and a sore throat and makes you feel poorly. When I grow up I want to be a nurse so I can nurse Papa when he's poorly.

Papa makes me say grace every mealtime and sometimes tells me a story at bedtime – that's seven o'clock. My favourite story is about 'Bung Yirds'. Now there's a bit of a puzzle for you Miss Burley. Then we say the Lord's Prayer together before he turns off the light and kisses me goodnight.

The End

Miss Burley was so impressed with Carice's portrait of her father that the poor child's task for the next holiday on the calendar was pretty well ordained.

LIFE WITH MAMA BY CARICE ELGAR

Mama is queen of the castle. You know who is king. That should make me a princess. But that would make Cook and Sarah the housemaid part of the Royal Family. Of course, this is nonsense. It's just that I spend most of my time with them – in the house that is. We don't speak much, but I listen. Sometimes they say funny things about Mama like what she would have on her gravestone – beside her name, that is. You will never guess. Well it was SHUSH! You should have seen them laugh. I laughed too. That made them stop. 'Mum's the word,' they said. What that meant I don't know – they talk different to Mama, more like Papa. Yesterday I asked Mama for a cat. 'Sly creatures,' she said, 'like some women I know,' she said it very quiet but I heard her. Then she said tut-tut and shook her head. I nearly asked her for a little dog but bit my tongue. We had a little dog when I was a baby. He was lovely and cuddly. He was always barking. Papa loved him. But he died. After that it was no more dogs. Mama won't allow them into the house – anyone's dog, even. Smelly things she calls them. I suppose they are but it's a nice smell. Papa thinks so too. Today he told me a secret and made me promise not to tell Mama. He is writing a piece of music about a dog. Isn't that fun.

Sometimes me and Mama go for walks to the post office even if it rains. I carry the parcels. They are very precious. Like gold, Mama says. They are Papa's music for his publishers. His publisher's name is Novello. Mama says the publishers are mean and don't pay Papa nearly enough, only two hundred pounds for a year's work. Though I must say it seems a lot to me. But Mama says we spent twice that much on paper and postage. I don't know why he goes to all the trouble then. All work and no pay makes Papa a sad boy. I never knew music was so heavy. It makes your arms ache, but Mama says it will make me strong.

Sometimes when Papa is working he won't even come down for dinner. So Sarah carries up a tray and leaves it outside the door of his study, and sometimes I have to sit and watch no mice nibble at his bread roll. Once Papa found me, I'd fallen asleep, waiting. Then he picked me up and cuddled me and kissed me all over. Mama saw and said he was spoiling me. It was the only time I ever saw him cross with Mama. Mama used to read me her poems but is far too busy these days looking after Papa. I liked them. She said she used to write books too.

Once Sarah the maid said it was a pity I didn't have a little brother or sister to play with. Then cook said Mama was past it. Past what? I said. But they just laughed, so I laughed too. It's Mama's birthday soon. I'm baking her a cake. It's a surprise. I hope I have room for all the candles.

The End

It was the first day of the new term at the Mount, and Elgar had just endured several hours of torture by an instrument more fiendish than any horror ever dreamed up by the Spanish Inquisition. It was, of course, the violin – which in the hands of heartless young ladies can cause pain that is past enduring. At least, that was his opinion.

Consequently, he was in no mood for socializing on receiving a request to take tea with the principal before going home.

'Sit down, Eddie, and let me pour you a cup of tea. You look absolutely buggered,' Rosa said as he entered.

'Just a quick one, if I may, love. I can't wait to get home and take a bath.'

Take a bath, thought Rosa. Alice has been at him again. Long ago on those vacations in Austria he used to say 'have a bath'. She had kept a mental list of the gradual upgrading of his vocabulary. It amused her enormously.

For a moment they sized each other up. To Rosa he was still as attractive as ever, if a little drawn. To Elgar the elfin creature masquerading as a head-mistress behind the massive desk seemed more seductive than ever – and equally dangerous.

'Don't tell me those outrageous little flirts haven't been practising in the holidays,' said Rosa, breaking the silence.

'I doubt they even took their instruments out of their cases,' said Elgar with a shrug. 'Very dispiriting.'

'Well, here's something to buck you up then; someone you know very well has been very industrious indeed.' And from a drawer she produced a little blue exercise book.

'Not something for me to mark before I go home, please, Rosa, dear. My eyes are giving me hell.'

'You just sit back and drink your tea; this is going to do you a world of good.'

'Very well, then,' said Elgar with a sigh, knowing when to give in gracefully to the inevitable.

'Good,' said Rosa as she settled back in her chair, opened the book and began to read. '"Our Mutual Friends by Carice Elgar".'

'Good God,' interrupted Elgar, letting his tea cup drop into its saucer. 'So that's what she was up to, scribbling away in the hols.'

'I set most of my girls a holiday task, and Carice is no exception. Now, no more interruptions, please.'

Elgar nodded his acquiescence and obediently resumed sipping his tea, while in a voice both mellow and musical Rosa took up reading where she'd left off.

'"When new friends come to the house they always ask two questions even before they come in the front door. Why is there a bell-tent with a Union Jack in the front garden and why is the house called Forli? Well, Forli was an Italian painter who painted little angels playing musical instruments. I expect it reminds Papa happily of school every time he sees it."'

'Like hell it does!' said Elgar with a deprecating laugh. 'I say, you don't think she's trying to be clever at my expense, do you?'

'Carice with a sense of irony . . . ?' said Rosa with a sly smile. 'Who knows? She's your child.'

'Hmm!' Elgar remarked ruminatively as Rosa read on.

'"Papa writes music in the bell-tent. No wonder some people take him for a soldier. He wrote a march for Queen Victoria's Jubilee in that tent. It was called the Imperial March. It's very loud."'

'Of course it's loud. It had to be. The old girl's as deaf as a post.'

Rosa smiled and continued reading. '"We have many friends. Mama's, Papa's and some mutual. So you see, most of my friends are grown-ups. I am also friendly with Sarah the housemaid and cook. But they are not friends because you can't be friends with servants. Here is a list of Papa's special friends. Stewart Powell, Richard Arnold, Isabel Fitton, who all play music in the house from time to time – oh, and Basil Nevison who plays the cello; then there's Mr Baxter Townsend who rides a tricycle and rings the bell all the time because he's deaf. Then there's the Hearty Old Fart."' Here Rosa paused and looked at Elgar quizzically.

'My secret nickname for August Jaeger, my music editor,' said Elgar by way of explanation. 'No one's supposed to know that. Naughty girl.'

'Mmm. "And pretty Dorabella who runs a ladies' orchestra, and William Baker, who invites Mama and Papa to his big house for social weekends. Then there's Mama, though I don't know if a wife counts as a friend, does she? And Papa, too. He's there because he's everybody's friend. I think that's all. Oh, how could I forget Dan, bulldog Dan. His music is very funny indeed. And I think really that is all. And there's also a friendly house. There are thirteen friends altogether – and one is secret. And secretly, I think that one is definitely me. But I expect Papa doesn't want to let on in case it looks like favouritism."' Here Rosa stopped reading and looked up. 'Is there some hidden truth in all this, or is the child fantasizing?'

Elgar looked uncomfortable. 'Well, it's true I'm writing a set of variations inspired by a few friends, yes. The child seems to have screwed her imagination to my list of thirteen subjects – damn, one has to watch what one leaves lying around, doesn't one? They're quite short, the variations – character studies, you know – right up your alley, Rosa, I dare say. Each done in a style the subject might have adopted themselves if they'd composed them. Not unlike your own delightfully wicked imitations . . . Remember the spot-on way you lampooned that barman?'

Rosa detected evasion and guessed that Elgar was not entirely at ease with the situation. 'Why didn't you tell me all this? Why did I have to find it out from your daughter?'

'And why did you set her to spy on me?'

'That's nonsense, and you still haven't answered my question.'

'Because I've been writing it in the holidays and this is my first day back. Give me a chance.'

'I was wondering why you made no attempt to see me.'

'I saw no one. I worked non-stop every day. Satisfied?'

'Partially,' she replied, before slyly posing the killer question. 'And is Carice the secret variation?'

'No, of course not,' said Elgar, immediately regretting it.

'Then I can only conclude it's me,' Rosa replied with a dangerous smile. For the very idea that she might be excluded was anathema to her.

'No . . . It's not you, Rosa,' admitted Elgar reluctantly.

'Are you sure?' she asked, giving him a chance to reconsider. 'I could quite understand you wanting to keep our association secret.'

For a moment Elgar considered lying, but that would fool her only until she actually heard the music, so instead he replied, 'There are certain musical references that are peculiar to one person alone.'

'What musical references?'

'It's by someone you cannot abide.'

'Not Mendelssohn,' said Rosa in mock disgust.

Elgar nodded. 'His overture Calm Sea and a Prosperous Voyage.'

Rosa looked puzzled for a moment but only for a moment. 'It's that little tart who left you at the altar and sailed away to Australia,' she said with a smirk.

'New Zealand,' corrected Elgar, somewhat abashed.

'So where does that leave me?' asked Rosa, ominously.

He was in a difficult position and would have to tread warily. 'It would have been the height of indiscretion to include you in the variations. Think of what it would do to poor Alice.'

'That didn't stop you including that little slut Dorabella, did it? And don't tell me you haven't been fucking her right under Alice's nose for years! You shit! Under the same roof.'

'In your dreams,' murmured Elgar, dropping his gaze as she continued to stare at him – until like a gift from heaven came an irrefutable alibi. 'You haven't asked me what theme the variations are based on,' he said mysteriously.

'So tell me – as if that makes any difference,' said Rosa, spoiling for a fight.

'The theme is the greatest secret of all,' continued Elgar, dropping his voice to a whisper. 'Nobody knows the nature of the theme because I have never divulged it, not to anyone. Those that have happened to hear rough sketches of the work played by me on the piano have made any number of wild guesses, from "Auld Lang Syne" to the "Song of the Volga Boatmen" – all nonsense. That it may not be a musical theme at all has never entered their minds. That is why I have called them the "Enigma" Variations.' Here he gave Rosa a look that, as far as she was concerned, explained everything. More than a reprieve, it earned a full pardon.

'When is the première?' she asked, quite mollified.

'It is not fixed yet, but you shall be there; never fear, my love.'

Rosa fairly basked in satisfaction – what further proof did she need that he still loved her?

'Thank you, Ed. Trust you to fool the bastards. It'll be our secret. Run along now and take your bath – you deserve it.'

Elgar blew her a kiss and hastily took his leave. She never suspected, poor dear, but the true identity of the 'Enigma' theme would go with him to the grave.

NINE

True Confessions

'*F*ORGIVE ME, FATHER, for I have sinned,' murmured Elgar in a confessional in Birmingham Oratory one windy autumn day in 1899.

'When did you last attend confession, my son?' responded the frail voice of the priest on the other side of the grille.

'Last Friday,' replied Elgar boldly. 'Since when, I have been guilty of unclean thoughts, Father . . .'

'Concerning a woman?' asked the priest.

'Concerning several women, Father,' he replied contritely. 'I was sorely tempted.'

'Do you ever say the Lord's Prayer?'

'Every night, Father, usually with my daughter.'

'Do you omit the seventh line, perchance?'

Elgar did some quick mental arithmetic and came up with 'Lead us not into temptation.' 'Certainly not, Father.'

'Then you are not praying hard enough, or God would have heard you. I fear you are neglecting your religious devotions, my son.'

'On the contrary, Father; I'm at them night and day.'

'Elucidate.'

'"The Dream of Gerontius", Cardinal Newman's divine poem of death and transfiguration, Father,' replied Elgar with passion. 'I study it night and day, I know it by heart, it's my new catechism. I know every line. Try me.'

But the priest, who was becoming increasingly impatient, put temptation behind him and remained silent.

Not so Elgar:

'Firmly I believe and truly
  God is three and God is one~
  And I next acknowledge duly
  Manhood taken by the son
  And I trust and hope most fully
  In that manhood crucified
  And each thought and deed unruly –'

'I absolve thee from thy sins,' interrupted the priest, wishing devoutly to be rid of him. 'For your penance, say three Our Fathers and three Hail Marys. Go and sin no more.'

'But I have more to confess, Father. Please hear me, please,' urged Elgar.

But the priest had fallen silent again, wondering if he should get the sacristan forcibly to evict this man.

In the meantime Elgar seized his opportunity. 'I confess that I'm here under false pretences, Father Bellasis. Knowing that you hold the copyright to the poem, I came here to seek permission to set "The Dream of Gerontius" to music.'

Father Bellasis, for indeed it was he, was stunned. The deranged man was none other than Edward Elgar, the talented composer from Malvern whose cantata 'The Light of Life' had impressed him deeply. He had heard rumours that the chairman of the prestigious Birmingham Music Festival had discussed the possibility of commissioning Elgar to compose a religious choral work but had no inkling as to the choice of subject matter.

'You may possibly be aware that no less a personage than Anton Dvořák made the same request twelve years ago; and I shall give you the same answer the Cardinal himself gave in 1885, shortly before his untimely death.'

'Then it's a "No",' cut in Elgar despondently.

'Cardinal Newman's poem has a strong Catholic flavour,' resumed Father Bellasis, 'including the doctrine of purgatory, which would simply not be acceptable to the general public – 99 per cent of whom are not only Protestant but bitterly opposed to what they look on as wanton idolatry.'

'You are thinking of the prayer to the Holy Virgin, I presume.'

'Correct, and as for the local chorus who would perform the work, I know from personal experience that more than a few are violently anti-Catholic.'

'There comes a time, Father, when we have to stand up and be counted,' replied Elgar resolutely. 'And what's more, there is a big wide world of music-lovers beyond these shores where Cardinal Newman's visionary masterpiece would be made welcome. In any case, great art transcends boundaries. Look at Verdi's wonderful Requiem, for example.'

'With respect, Verdi has achieved greatness; you merely aspire to it.'

'That's not entirely correct, Father. None other than Carl Richter has premièred my variations in London and is planning to perform them at the Upper Rhine Festival in the spring.'

'Be ever watchful for the sin of pride, my son,' warned the priest balefully, before continuing on a slightly more positive note. 'I heard your "Enigma" Variations at New Brighton under the baton of Granville Bantock. And though I question your judgement in setting the antics of a bulldog to music, I admit to finding the "Nimrod" Variation quite sublime. Such profundity is rare in music. Who was the subject again?'

'His name is August Jaeger, Father. He is my music editor at Novello's.'

'According to your musical portrait, he must cut a truly noble figure, my son.'

'He's five feet three, squints, sports a walrus moustache, suffers from asthma – and has an appalling accent.'

'Then he must possess a pure and noble soul, this Jaeger.'

'That's why you must give me permission to write "Gerontius",' urged Elgar. 'He, too, has a nobility of spirit. Let me set his journey to his Maker to music. I feel everything I have worked on so far is but a prelude to this moment. For years it has been my ambition – ever since I received a copy of the poem as a gift on my wedding day. I understand this man. I am this man!'

'Are you not forgetting Gerontius is a sinner?'

'Like I said, I am Gerontius,' replied Elgar, simply.

'That you understand your fellow man is abundantly clear from the friends pictured within your Variations – they have humour, love, compassion and even an element of mystery. Tell me, do you ever suffer doubts: does your faith ever waver? Are you anything less than devout?' questioned the priest.

'To tell you the truth, Father,' said Elgar, sounding a note of despondency, 'as a good Catholic I'm really God-awful.'

This pulled the Reverend Father up short. By his own admission Elgar was a bad Catholic: vain, arrogant and big on blasphemy. As to the possibility of his turning out a work that would bring everlasting glory to the Catholic faith, he had very little going for him.

'Then give me one good reason why I should give you my blessing?' said the priest, beginning to tire of the encounter.

'Well, if nothing else,' said Elgar philosophically, 'it could win us a couple of converts, and heaven knows we need 'em.'

Then in the darkness of the confessional Father Bellasis, in spite of the peril to his immortal soul, gave a chuckle. The sound illuminated Elgar with a ray of hope.

TEN

Post Mortem

O VER DRINKS WITH Elgar in her study a few days later Rosa shook her head incredulously and said, 'Why on earth didn't you write to the old boy instead of putting yourself through all that misery in the confessional? I'm surprised you can still remember what one looks like.'

'Waiting for a reply to the letter would have been sheer torture,' said Elgar. 'One more rejection slip and I'd do away with myself, I swear it. If I had a pound for every rejection I've ever had, I'd be a very rich man today, believe me.'

'How much are you getting paid for it?' asked Rosa bluntly.

'Two hundred pounds cash in hand and a pittance for royalties.'

'And how long will it take to compose?'

'Well, the première is scheduled for early October – so, barely six months. I'll have to get a move on.'

'That must be a pound a day. In three weeks or so you'll be able to afford a bicycle,' said Rosa brightly. 'Then you can really get a move on.'

'I say. Do you still have those bicycle catalogues handy?'

'I've been keeping them in mothballs,' said Rosa, opening a drawer and placing a couple on the desk before her.

'Splendid,' he exclaimed, getting up and standing behind her with a hand on her shoulder.

'You have choices,' said Rosa, placing one hand over his and turning the illustrated pages with the other.

'I like the look of that one,' said Elgar, as a sturdy machine named the Royal Sunbeam was revealed.

'You'll be king of the road on that model, Ted, and all for twenty-odd quid. The only snag is, it's got a fixed wheel.'

'What's the alternative?'

'Why, a free wheel, of course, which means that when you're going down-hill you don't have to keep pedalling.'

'That would make me feel very unsafe. Any other choices?'

'Well,' said Rosa, opening the other catalogue, 'you could always go for a tandem.'

Elgar studied an engraving of a bicycle built for two and shook his head. 'That would mean I'd always have to take Alice along.'

'You don't have to take Alice along,' said Rosa meaningfully, staring at the page as though her pointed remark were a casual suggestion.

'People would talk,' said Elgar, getting her drift and kissing her on the back of her neck.

'I know these roads like the back of my hand,' said Rosa, more insistently. 'I could show you around.'

'Does that mean I'd have to take a back seat?'

'Just think of the wonderful view you'd have . . . of my ass,' she said with a cheeky smile.

'That could lead to, um . . . sartorial embarrassment on my part. I may not be able to contain myself,' he replied with a wicked grin.

'Don't worry.' Rosa turned to a page of cycling accessories. 'That eventuality has been taken care of. Here – listen to this. "Male Modesty in the Saddle . . . May we offer a word of advice to our growing list of gentlemen customers who may be new to the delights of the fastest-growing social activity in this country today and who are desirous of cycling in mixed company. As yet, you may not be aware of certain precautions that need to be taken if decorum is to be maintained at all times. Female riders should not continue beyond this point, which is strictly for the benefit of male novitiates.

'"For those uninformed beginners, we highly recommend the purchase of a pair of Crosby's plus-fours-plus. These high-quality knickerbockers have a quantity of extra material let into the area around the crotch, where the steady pumping action of the nether limbs in the close proximity of the male member is apt to give rise to stimulation, which would otherwise soon become all too evident to the weaker sex – thus causing not only considerable embarrassment but also the real possibility of a serious accident.'"

At this Rosa turned to Elgar, who overcame his mute astonishment to blurt out, 'Why on earth didn't you tell me all this before? I'd have taken it up ages ago!'

In the event, Elgar was not to invest in the Royal Sunbeam for some time. Instead he hired an inferior machine from a local ironmonger, who also gave him lessons. He wasn't sure he really wanted to commit to this new hobby, despite the obvious perks referred to in the catalogues – though he did lash out for a pair of Crosby's plus-fours-plus, for fear of offending Alice.

She, too, was tempted to sample life on the open road and went one better than Edu, hiring a machine with three wheels rather than two. The built-in stability of the design enabled her to hit the road earlier than her adventurous husband with his precarious perch, though there soon came a day when Alice was able to record a very significant event in her diary, which read: 'E can now go beautifully.' (Note that Alice, having so far been unable to improve appreciably Elgar's speech habits, had chosen to satirize them, in the hope that this tactic prove more effectual. And, to a certain extent, her method actually worked.)

Significantly, Elgar penned the last note of Gerontius on the same day. It was 3 August 1891; the location was an isolated gamekeeper's cottage that Elgar had rented called 'Birchwood'. Alice was present when he wrote a few lines of Ruskin's on the last page of the score. 'This is the best of me, for the rest I ate, and drank and slept, loved and hated another; my life was as the vapour and is not; but this I saw and knew; this, if anything of mine, is worth your memory.'

However, the majority of the audience at the first performance in Birmingham, just two months later, were of a contrary opinion – including Rosa. Both she and Elgar held a post-mortem in her office at the Mount, in what was to have been an intimate champagne celebration. Fittingly, the champagne proved rather flat.

'Bloody chorus didn't know the words,' Elgar moaned.

'I hear their music was late in arriving.'

'Bloody printers were late with the proofs. The sudden death of the chorus-master didn't help. And his replacement, who hated me, had one foot in the grave.'

'So did your Gerontius – quite fitting, considering he was playing a dying man. As for the Angel of the Agony, agony is what we were all made to suffer. And more than once, he actually lost his voice.'

'More's the pity he ever found it again,' lamented Elgar. 'The Guardian Angel had no voice to lose, poor love.'

'The conductor was a disaster. He never realized the complexity of the score until it was too late. You really needed twice the rehearsal time.'

'I've worked hard for forty years, and at last Providence denies me a decent hearing of my work,' moaned Elgar, sinking into self-pity. 'I always said God was against art, and I still believe it.'

'No doubt I'd sympathize, my love, if I shared your beliefs; but like most of the audience I found Cardinal Newman's concept of God quite repugnant!'

'Be careful what you say. The Cardinal and I are of the same opinion.'

'Very well, I'll shut up.'

'No, go ahead. Speak up, woman. If you represent the general consensus, I'd better hear the worst. Be the devil's advocate, by all means.'

'Very well,' said Rosa, taking a gulp of her flat champagne. 'Here goes. To be perfectly honest, I just don't see how you could promote that liturgical horror story in the first place. Cardinal Newman at his most pious, serving up the same tripe the priests have always dished out to frighten us into submission. "You must cringe before thy Maker: sorry, God, sorry, God", in hope of a reprieve at death from – what? Death? No, Gerontius is already dead. His fear is of missing his glimpse of God, even though the Angel warns him it's going to burn him alive – that searing glance. Well, I'd stay clear of that one.

'"Don't worry," says the Angel, "you can always ask Jesus to intercede on your behalf; he knows what it is like to be torn to shreds." But no, Gerontius begs to be admitted into the presence of giant God on his giant throne, with all kinds of puffed-up idiots larking about him, telling him, "Oh yes, you're God, you're the best; do burn us up and then heal us; you're so good at that, tra-la-la." It's a sado-masochistic orgy.

'And lest Gerontius ever feel relaxed for one minute, even in death, or feel he might finally be all right – there at the door to God's majesty are these sarky little demons who hiss nasty insults at captive souls, whose big crime was to sing in church but not sing loud enough; I mean, it's not like they'd killed anyone! Just been a bit hypocritical and yawned behind their prayer books while putting a good face on it all. Well, what else could you do? Caught like a fly in amber between the stern disapproval of the priests and God himself. I mean, is nothing good enough for God?

'God burns you with his glance, yes, but if you're cringing enough he might allow you to stay and sing love songs to him. And that's the good news! First you get to be "washed clean" by being thrown to the bottom of a lake and left to contemplate your wormhood for an eternity or two. Well, you can keep your God of worms!'

'Perhaps I should set your version to music,' said Elgar, dangerously calm.

'Let me hear your interpretation of the poem first,' said Rosa, pouring another glass of champagne to steady her nerves, for she was shaking like a leaf.

He saw this and realized what it had cost her. Used to unqualified praise from his friends, this was like summer rains – unexpectedly refreshing.

'The music, of course, is magnificent; you've surpassed yourself and Verdi, too, come to that,' added Rosa. 'But the text, Eddie; the text . . .'

'Frankly, I find it refreshingly soothing,' Elgar began. 'It addresses an inner state – the approach of an unreasoning ecstasy and bliss. That's all angels are: the personification of an inner sense of joy. Like my music, the journey of Gerontius through the realms of hell and heaven proclaims the infusion of a palpable bliss that acknowledges, but makes unimportant, all pain – physical, emotional . . . even the pain of hearing someone you admire scold you like you're a stupid schoolboy.'

Rosa blushed, but Elgar half smiled.

He continued, 'I find the Guardian Angel's reassurances touching and cheering. If anything, she wants to remove Gerontius's guilt, rather than reinforce it – and talk him gently through the encounter with fire and water and fear and despair that Gerontius's soul goes through as it sheds its identification with the lesser body left on earth.'

Here Rosa felt bound to protest. 'With friends and family adding their own prayers all around the bed – "Oh, spare him, God, do." Hardly a celebration of a man's life. I'd like to see you celebrate a man's life, instead of making excuses for it, Eddie – something fresh and invigorating, something to blow away that clinging stink of incense.'

'I'd like to see that myself,' said Elgar, pulling her close to him and staring deep into her soft brown eyes. 'Let's go to bed.'

ELEVEN

A Bicycle Built for Two

*T*HE VERY NEXT day at the school the youngest member of the family also stood face to face with Miss Burley, who was more than a little apprehensive; and after Carice's message, 'Mama wants to see you straight away', became even more so.

Rosa's mind raced as she pedalled at a funeral pace to what she often looked upon as 'the mausoleum' – a feeling confirmed by Alice opening the door to her knock and going, 'Shush!'

Moments later in the drawing-room Rosa waited breathlessly for Alice to speak. After what seemed like an age, she did so, in whispers.

'Edu is in total despair. Today he received a letter from Cambridge offering him a degree.'

'You mean they want to make him a Doctor of Music? That's wonderful!' gushed Rosa, suddenly free of all feelings of guilt. 'At last he's getting the recognition he deserves.' She hastily added, 'You must be so proud.'

'Please let me finish,' admonished Alice, with a glint in her eye. 'At this very minute he is upstairs penning a refusal.'

'What?' said Rosa, suddenly transfixed.

'He says we can't afford to buy the ceremonial robes. I've tried to reason with him, but he simply won't listen to me.'

Rosa hesitated only a second before bounding from the room and racing upstairs to the study. Elgar was licking an envelope as she burst in unannounced.

'Did you see the sign on the door?' he barked.

'Yes,' said Rosa, suddenly abashed.

'What did it say?'

'Please knock.'

'Then kindly do so, and make it quick. I'm just off to the post office.'

For a moment Rosa made as if to comply, then on a sudden impulse grabbed the letter from his hands, tore it to shreds, threw it in his face, burst into tears and ran out of the room and down the stairs, shouting, 'You don't have to buy the robes, you stupid old Scrooge; you can hire the fuckers.'

Everyone in the house heard her loud and clear, from Cook in the kitchen to Lady Monica Willoughby-Smythe, who had just been admitted by Sarah the maid. While in the drawing-room Alice, shamed to the depths of her being, considered slashing her wrists with a paperknife.

As for Elgar upstairs in his study, well, he, poor man, didn't know whether to laugh or cry. Forget the f—ing robes. Was this the end of a 'beautiful friendship' or the beginning of something far deeper?

Fittingly enough, it was the Royal Sunbeam that played a big part in the outcome. Elgar finally bit the bullet and splashed out on a brand-new model, an extravagance made possible only because a group of friends had a whip-round and raised the necessary forty-five pounds to set Elgar up in full Cambridge regalia, mortar-board and all. So not only was he geared up to receive his doctorate he was also ready to explore the mysteries beyond the confines of Malvern.

And who better to show him the way than the knowledgeable Rosa? She could also lead him astray, thought Alice, unaware of their close relationship but fully conscious of the potential dangers – which is why their first cycling excursion was a threesome and why there were three potential destinations.

Rosa suggested Upton-upon-Severn, only a few miles away, with a very good pub on the river. Alice opted for Worcester and the shops.

'That's rather far, old girl, for a first go, you know. How about dropping in on Mum and Dad?' suggested Elgar. 'It's on the way, and if you feel like pressing on we've got the option – they'd love to see us.'

'And you can tell them the good news about Cambridge,' said Alice.

'Splendid!' said Rosa, putting a bold face on it. She'd been outvoted, but her time would come. In any case, there would be compensations. Alice was never completely at ease in the company of the worthy old couple, and it would be fun to see her slumming and pretending to love it.

Then her face clouded over, for there – cycling towards them – was a very pretty girl, smiling and waving and riding with no hands. The last time she had bumped into 'the slut', as Rosa was wont to think of her, the girl had been lying under the trees with Elgar at Birchwood. Cow! She was the tenth variation of the 'Enigma', and her name was Dora Penny (cheap at double the price). But since the popularity of Elgar's catchy little tune personifying her, she had become universally known as 'Dorabella'. Though, since Elgar had once spoken admiringly of her delightful little tummy, Rosa had secretly rechristened her 'Adorabelly'. Bitch!

Alice smiled to herself. She despised them both.

Dorabella was quite a woman. Still barely twenty, she was the daughter of a widowed clergyman. Her father's remarriage to a dear friend of Alice's established a connection with the Elgars. In frequent visits to Forli – 'to see Alice', as propriety would have it – the young woman had rapidly fallen under Elgar's spell. She began regularly cycling the forty miles from her home in Wolverhampton just to be at his side, a feat of endurance that spoke volumes about her feelings. He found himself encouraging her. She was extremely musical – she ran a ladies' orchestra – and only twenty years of age, for goodness' sake. He admired her.

Naturally, both Rosa and Alice were jealous as hell. But as far as the latter was concerned there were certain advantages to the obvious attraction.

Dorabella always put Edu in a good mood whenever she came to stay – and everyone benefited from that. She also got him out of the house so that Alice could get on with planning Edu's conducting engagements, which were becoming frequent. It took considerable application to handle his growing business affairs, and with which he couldn't be bothered.

Pity the creature was so pretty, though – and could talk Edu's own language like a professional. By comparison, Alice was only an amateur; and as she knew only too well, Edu had no time whatsoever for amateurs, no time at all.

Dorabella's presence was equally challenging to Rosa, who had secret designs on her unsuspecting man. Yes, she would marry her Teddy one day; and the sooner the better. She doubted that Elgar would ever divorce Alice – it simply wasn't done, and the fact that he was a Catholic exacerbated matters. But Alice couldn't last for ever. Just look at her: frail, anaemic and since the recent operation on her throat looking more like a wizened old shrew than ever. If she could be persuaded to take up tricycling seriously she was quite likely to drop dead on the first Malvern Hill she encountered. Which was – truth to tell – the prime reason Rosa had suggested the strenuous ride.

'I've got a tune that'll knock 'em flat,' bragged Elgar. 'I'll play it to you when we get back.'

'Sing it to me, sing it to me now,' pleaded Dorabella.

'Why not,' replied Elgar, pleased to be on the move at last. 'Here we go, for the first public performance of my Pomp and Circumstance March No. 1.'

'Oh, please, Edu,' gasped Alice between puffs, 'not in front of all these people.' In the distance a well-attended cricket match had caught her eye.

'Nonsense,' said Elgar. 'If ever I wrote a tune for the people, this is the one, believe me!'

'Does that include local people?' queried Alice.

'Local people, London people. People of England, Ireland, Scotland and Wales and the whole wide world.' Whereupon, he pom-pommed his way through the most famous tune he would ever write, so catchy that by the third repeat the two girls could also join in.

So by the time they passed the county cricket grounds they were all singing to the skies – except for Alice, who pedalled doggedly on, head down, hoping against hope that Lady Monica Willoughby-Smythe and His Lordship, who was chairman of the cricket club, were not in attendance. Whether or not her personal fears of exposure were justified, there were many in the crowd on that historic day who did take notice, thinking, That's a catchy tune. And, as Elgar had prophesied, the approval would grow. Once the words 'Land of Hope and Glory' were stuck on no one would ever forget it. Across time and landscape the tune stretched, even to the ears of every benighted high-school student in the United States of America of the twentieth and twenty-first centuries, for whom its tune would for ever mark the march down the aisle to collect a diploma.

Fifteen minutes later the chorus of three were ready to whet their whistles and Alice was ready to rest her weary limbs, so the appearance of the Cross Keys at Powick was a very welcome sight. But when it came to take their leave an hour later the sight that met their eyes was anything but. It was drizzling.

Consternation and a quick confab. To go on or back? Go back before it gets any worse was the general consensus. So with spirits somewhat dampened they pointed their machines towards Malvern and set off. This time there was no singing, for which Alice was extremely grateful. Everyone was sunk in their own thoughts – clouded by a surfeit of cider that was far stronger than it seemed. Indeed, legend had it that the reason the local lunatic asylum seemed excessively large for such a sparsely populated area was entirely down to the mind-fuddling effects of the local cider.

Elgar, not surprisingly perhaps, recalled the days when he was bandmaster at the Powick asylum and softly hummed La Blonde, the tune he'd written as therapy for the inmates. It was inspired and dedicated to the lovely Helen Weaver (Heaven-Weaver, he called her) who retained the power to haunt him despite the efforts of the present company, God bless 'em. Dorabella was ruminating on how to get the better of 'Burly Miss Burley' as she had secretly christened her. Miss Burley was planning to invite Teddy – and Teddy alone – to her holiday cottage in Wales. Bedraggled Alice's plans did not go beyond a hot bath the minute she got back home. Any others could wait.

Then Elgar got a puncture . . . whereupon the stupid idiot who invented the pneumatic tyre was cursed with every cuss word in Elgar's extensive German vocabulary. And though the little group had heard most of it before, Alice crossed herself and earnestly prayed that a group of passing nuns were bliss-fully ignorant of that highly expressive and rather brutal language.

Both girls carried puncture outfits in their saddlebags but lacked the bowl of water necessary to find the offending leak. No doubt the nearby convent would oblige, but Elgar was in no mood to hang about, so permission was obtained from the Mother Superior to house Mr Phoebus (as the Royal Sunbeam had been christened) until it could be collected by a local carrier at a later date.

That settled, all that remained was to get home and dry. Various solutions were proposed, but only one was practical: two people would have to take the tricycle – but which two? Since Elgar steadfastly refused to be seen riding a lady's bicycle, that meant he had no option. And, since Alice could not manage a two-wheeler, she also had no choice. And, since she could barely get herself along, let alone a passenger, she was obliged to stand on the axle casing behind her husband and hang on for dear life while he did the pedalling.

The indignity of it was almost too much for Alice to bear, but the rain was intensifying, leaving no alternative. So off they went down a slight incline, which enabled Elgar to get up quite a head of steam. The only one who didn't see the funny side of it was Alice.

Elgar thought it was a huge joke. His sense of humour regained and mind-ful of the figure poor Alice was cutting, he burst into song again. The choice? It was obvious – one might almost say inevitable: that poem of praise to the warrior ladies riding through Richard Wagner's 'Valhalla' to the irresistible strains of the 'Ride of the Valkyries'. And once again the two young women, seeing themselves as fearless heroines mounted on trusty steeds, joined in the stirring chorus. And this time there was no la-la-ing, for they'd all been to *Der Ring des Nibelungen* on a summer holiday in Stuttgart and knew the words (in German, of course) off by heart. And the harder it rained, the louder they sang. 'Hoyotoho! Hoyotoho! Heraha! Heraha!' and so on, *ad infinitum*.

And just as everyone had got into the swing of things they came in sight of the cricket ground where rain had just stopped play. And there, horror of horrors, were Lord and Lady Willoughby-Smythe driving towards them in an open Landau.

The next few minutes were the very worst in Alice's life – worse than toothache, oral sex or even childbirth. What sins could she have committed that the Almighty would punish her thus? The dignitaries could barely believe their eyes. They had always considered the Major-General's daughter teetering on the eccentric, but this convinced them that she had finally toppled over. And for this they blamed the husband, singing an ugly guttural German *lied*, along with two concubines he flouted shamelessly in public – while forcing his good woman to ride on the back of a tricycle like a common urchin.

To her credit, Alice carried off the encounter shrouded in the shreds of her dignity. She even managed a gracious smile and a royal wave, which caused His Lordship, who knew nothing of German mythology, to remark, as he raised his topper, 'She only needs a trident to pass muster as Queen Boadicea.'

To which Her Ladyship replied, as she graciously acknowledged Alice's inappropriate salutation, 'Quite, my dear, but she's heading in the wrong direction.'

'I don't follow you, my dear,' replied His Lordship. 'Wrong direction?'

'She's going away from the Powick madhouse – she should be heading straight for it.'

'Non-stop,' quipped His Lordship.

TWELVE

The Peerage Postponed

*T*HE CHARACTERS PRIVILEGED to hear that magnificent tune on a rainy August day in 1901 were not the only ones to recognize its merits. In fact, when King Edward VII first encountered it, all dressed up in its dazzling orchestral finery, he requested – nay, demanded – that it be included in the Coronation ode that Elgar had been commissioned to write in honour of the illustrious occasion. For along with the twentieth century, the demise of Victoria and the prospect of a revolutionary new era, Elgar had finally arrived with a bang.

Simultaneously, the press arrived on his doorstep – and not only the local press, either.

'The gentleman from London is at the door, master,' announced Sarah. Shall I show him in?'

Elgar, adjusting his cravat, nodded to Sarah's reflection in the drawing-room mirror.

'Right away, Sarah. I am expecting him.'

A moment later a flashy young man in spats, bow-tie and bowler entered the room, removed his hat and introduced himself.

'Miles Spooner, *London Morning News*, Mr Elgar. Pleased to meet you.'

'It's Doctor,' said Elgar, correcting him.

'Doctor?' queried the journalist.

'And a very good doctor he is, too,' piped Carice, popping up from behind the settee.

'And are you one of his patients, young lady?' asked Spooner with a grin.

'When my dolly broke her leg the doctor mended it with glue.'

'So you have more than one string to your bow – if you'll excuse the pun, Dr Elgar,' said Spooner with a self-satisfied smirk.

'Run along, Fish-face,' admonished Elgar. 'We have some serious business to conduct.'

'*Molto allegro*,' added Spooner, producing a notepad and pencil and taking a seat unbidden. 'I understand you are rather pressed for time, Dr Elgar. Oh, and Fish-face,' crooned Spooner to Carice on her way out, 'be a dear and hang around ... by the pond. I'd like to take a picture of you with the Doctor before I go – and see if you can find that doll with the broken leg and a tube of glue.'

Carice laughed at the funny man in the bow-tie and left the room, leaving Spooner facing a frosty paterfamilias.

'Is it a trout your daughter puts you in mind of, Doctor – or is it a cod or perhaps a catfish or even ... ?'

'That will do,' interrupted Elgar. 'I must ask you to kindly leave my house.'

'Please, Dr Elgar, forgive me. I breakfasted too early on my way down from London. Let's start afresh, please! I was only trying to be sociable.'

There was a pause as Elgar decided to give him the benefit of the doubt.

Looking contrite, Spooner prepared to put the boot in. 'Tell me, how must it feel to stand in Westminster Abbey as the choir and orchestra perform your tribute to the King in the company of your peers, Dr Elgar? Famous men like Sir Edward German, Sir Frederick Bridge, Sir Hubert Parry and Sir Arthur Sullivan ... How does it feel to know that all these musical knights of the realm – resplendent in their robes of ermine – have been passed over in favour of a humble shopkeeper's son from Worcester, dressed in cap and gown, thanks entirely to a timely act of charity?'

Elgar saw he had been set up but decided to play the game. 'I have no idea. It never crossed my mind,' he began. 'But now that you have put the notion into my head, I suppose I might feel like Cinderella in her rags being favoured by the handsome prince over her ugly sisters for the ultimate prize, despite all their finery and very best efforts.'

Spooner blinked. He was rather impressed by the analogy. 'Cinderella also won a title, Dr Elgar. What would you say to a knighthood?'

'Knighthood? Did someone mention a knighthood?' remarked Alice, entering the room.

Elgar made the introductions and concluded with 'Mr Spooner was asking if I'd accept a knighthood in the event of one being offered, my dear. What say you?'

'I say, keep your own council, Edu, for whatever you say to this individual will be taken down and used in evidence against you. I think it's time you were leaving, young man and – strictly off the record – whether he ever makes the honours list or not, Elgar was born one of nature's knights and he will undoubtedly die one. Good-day.'

Spooner pulled a face as he rammed his hat on, pausing in the doorway to remark, 'I was wondering, Mrs Elgar, exactly what kind of fish Fish-face is?'

Without missing a beat, Alice replied, 'Why, a goldfish, of course. And, judging from your behaviour, it's perfectly obvious that you are a very common sea urchin.'

An hour later on their way to Stretton-Grandison, a picturesque village on the road to Hereford, Rosa had to smile in spite of herself as Elgar recounted the morning's events at home. She had a sneaking regard for Alice despite not wishing her well.

But Rosa was, determined not to let any softening towards Alice spoil their outing. This was to be their last ride together before the Elgars set off for London and certain fame first thing on the morrow, the eventful 26 June 1902.

Over cider and baps at the village inn they chatted excitedly about the recent success of Elgar's new overture Cockaigne – In London Town. What a vibrant, kaleidoscopic musical picture it was.

'It's the sort of thing Richard Strauss might have written if he'd been born a Londoner,' enthused Rosa.

'Or a Worcesterer,' added Elgar.

'He's already conducted it in Berlin – to great acclaim, I hear. Perhaps it'll inspire him to write a symphonic portrait of the German capital, though it would never be half so exciting. Oh, I do love that moment when the lovers strolling in the park sneak into a church and hold hands in the shadows. It so reminds me of us, Ted.'

'But we've never been to London together.'

'But we've been in plenty of churches, holding hands in the shadows. Upton, Hadley, Pershore, Cradley.'

'You're wandering,' said Elgar, not wanting to get maudlin. 'Get back to London, what else do you see?'

Her eyes sparkled. 'I see brass bands, marching off to bash the Boers.'

'And the lament for those who won't be coming back,' said Elgar with a touch of pathos. 'Don't forget that. It's crucial.'

'So's the merry-go-round of Piccadilly Circus. Horses' hooves, the shouts of cabbies, the whirling wheels, the cries of the costers, the laughs of the painted women, the flash of the silver-topped canes of the toffs, the hell-for-leather roar of the *hoi polloi* . . .'

'Stop, you're making me dizzy,' gasped Elgar.

'I thought that was the general idea,' laughed Rosa.

'I'm exhausted. Let's have another drink.'

A pint later, Rosa became more reflective. 'Pity about Gerontius.'

'What do you mean? Performances in Germany, France, America, here, there and everywhere, even in Worcester. What more do you want?'

'Why did you do it, Ted?'

'Do what?'

'Cut out all the Catholic bits.'

'That's a hell of an exaggeration, my girl,' protested Elgar. 'Just a few Josephs, a handful of Holy Virgins, a couple of martyred saints and a little bit of purgatory, if I remember rightly. It was either cut it or forget it! After all, Worcester is a C of E cathedral. You can always tell a Protestant church – the real Presence is conspicuous by its absence. One day it will all be different.'

'One day pigs may fly,' said Rosa cynically, 'and a Catholic might be knighted.'

'Funny you should say that,' mused Elgar.

'If it's on the cards, Ted, would you accept it?'

'Is the Pope Catholic? If I refused, it would be over dear Alice's dead body.'

'The King's got to 'ave 'is appendix out – the Coronation's orf!' proclaimed a voice from the blue, which proved to be that of a postman.

Rosa and Elgar exchanged looks – each waiting for the other to speak.

'That means the trip to London is off,' said Elgar finally, with mock solemnity. 'Poor Alice. It'll kill her. Do you know what this means, my girl?'

'It means we can spend the entire summer together,' said Rosa, reaching across the table and taking his hand. 'Just the two of us.'

When Alice heard the shocking news she immediately had a fit of the vapours and took to her bed.

THIRTEEN

Sir Ted

*A*WEEK LATER ALICE got up, put her court dress in mothballs and set about making her dreams come true. To start with, she made it her business to attend every concert and gala that was going and to rub shoulders with all the movers and shakers who really mattered in the world of music.

She also put on her metaphorical mountaineering boots and by indefatigable social climbing finally conquered the heights of the nobility – with the result that in two years almost to the day that long-awaited letter arrived offering her dear Edu a knighthood.

And, after Alice, who was the first to know? Well, it was a little old man with a weathered face and wispy white hair who might have been taken for a farm labourer prematurely aged by a lifetime's exposure to the raging elements. In fact, he was not a true son of the soil at all but a retired shopkeeper of seventy-three, prematurely aged, yes, but dignified with it.

And the day that his honoured son cycled the twenty-odd miles from his home in Malvern to blow his own trumpet and herald the news Elgar senior was staying at a cottage called 'The Elms', Stoke Prior, near Bromsgrove, the home of his daughter Polly – Edward's sister – and her family.

After a good meal washed down with plenty of strong cider cousin Julie, a keen amateur photographer, cajoled Elgar and his dad away from their cups and into the garden to immortalize the event of which they were all so proud with her plate camera.

'Polly, give me the programme. I want to hold the programme,' insisted the old man.

'It won't show up,' protested Julie. 'It's too small. Now, sit in this chair and don't fuss.'

'A three-day festival at Covent Garden of Eddie's music in front of the King and Queen is anything but small, my girl. You're talking about twelve solid hours of music with two hundred and fifty singers and an orchestra of more than a hundred,' piped up Grandad, taking a seat. 'Did you get to sit in the Royal Box with the King and Queen, son?'

'No, Father. I was conducting. But I did dine with the King and the Prince of Wales at Buckingham Palace.'

'Without Alice?' the aged parent asked in astonishment.

'No, of course not. Alice was in attendance the entire time. It was she who was largely responsible for the festival in the first place.'

'I suppose I shall have to call her Your Ladyship from now on,' said the old man resignedly.

'No, of course not, Father.'

'Does she have a lady-in-waiting? And do you have a footman, son? You both deserve it.'

'No, we do not,' said Elgar.

'But he does have a valet to dress him. Don't you, Your Lordship?' said Polly, who had just come into the garden with a jug of lemonade, which she began serving with a mock servility.

'A valet to dress him?' said the old man, quite concerned. 'Have you hurt yourself, son?'

Everyone ignored this.

'And you'll have to address His Lordship as Sir Ted and bow every time you speak to him,' added Julie, entering into the fun. 'And you always have to ask permission to sit in his presence, don't forget.'

'That's called etiquette,' said Polly.

'All right, ladies, you've had your little joke,' said Elgar. 'Let's get it over with.'

'I remember now. Yes, etiquette, in the homes of the high and mighty, tuning their pianos,' cut in the old man eagerly. 'Never speak unless you're spoken to, wipe your feet, wear nice clean gloves and keep your eyes to yourself. I know my place, Sir Teddy, don't worry,' he continued, struggling to his feet and bowing deeply.

'Oh, do sit down. We're losing the light,' said Julie, hoping to dispel the growing sense of discomfort.

'I hear you're moving tomorrow, Eddie,' said Polly, trying to maintain normality. 'To Hereford. Is that right?'

'Sir Eddie to you, my girl,' cut in the old man.

'Yes . . . No . . .' said Elgar, getting flustered. 'Actually, we're going on the 26th.'

'And will you be taking your grand piano with you, Your Lordship?' asked the old man innocently, still mindful of etiquette.

For a moment Elgar wondered if the old man was having him on but concluded that he was simply overwhelmed and confused by it all. He looked more fragile than the last time they had met. 'Yes, of course, Father. It's a fine instrument, naturally.'

'Then it's sure to need tuning on arrival, sir,' the old man added. 'In which case, may I recommend Elgar Brothers of number 10, the High Street, Worcester, piano tuners by appointment to the nobility, including Major-General Roberts of Redmarley. I'll take my boots off at the back door as usual, Your Lordship, don my kid gloves and keep my head down, my eyes to myself and only speak when I am spoken to. May I assume I have your valued custom, Your Lordship?'

No one knew where to look. The joke had gone sour.

'Come, let's get it over with quickly. I must be on my way before it gets dark,' muttered Elgar, shaken by the decline in his father's condition. The women, too, were disturbed.

Julie sprang into action. 'Watch the birdie,' she called, as father and son froze for a second and – click! – it was all over, thank God.

And as Elgar pedalled away swiftly into the enveloping dusk, distressed and wretched, he steeled himself not to look over his shoulder for fear the old man would still be at the gate, continually bowing, as he had been when Elgar bade a hasty goodbye. He should have seen more of him, the dear old soul, but lately Elgar's growing fame had made ever-increasing demands on his time. He was rarely in the same place two days running.

For apart from the social treadmill, which Alice had at last convinced him was essential to his career, he was touring with the London Symphony Orchestra as resident conductor – whenever he wasn't abroad conducting his own works in Europe and America. And he hadn't rested on his laurels, either. Two more Pomp and Circumstances marches had followed in the wake of the illustrious first; while another oratorio, *The Apostles*, and a big orchestral work, *In the South* – which had been premièred at the Covent Garden Festival with the composer conducting – had all added to his growing stature.

England's greatest living composer had at last been acknowledged by the establishment and the great British public alike. As to his private life, his family and friends, well . . . Pity about his dear old dad. He owed him everything.

As a boy he'd had the run of the music shop, with free access to scores and instruments alike. That's where he learned to strum a piano and play pizzicato on a violin. And to attend church regularly every Sunday, to watch Dad play the organ and have a go himself, until he became proficient enough to deputize whenever Dad decided to pop across to the Woolpack to wet his whistle.

Thoughts of parental inevitably led to memories of Anne, his adored mother, who had passed away a few years previously. How he missed her. At the time of her death the realization that he had not seen her for an entire year shook him.

The occasion had been a memorable one. It was early December 1901. He had gathered up the robes that marked the realization of his Cambridge Doctorate, newly delivered only the day before, and carted them to Worcester to show the proud old couple. He still vividly recalled how moved he had been by their overwhelming delight. This was tangible proof of their dear son's recognition.

And as he pedalled on, his eyes moistened as he remembered the way Anne had gently smoothed the material with her weathered hand, as if it were a living thing – and had nearly gone mad when Dad, in toasting his brilliant son's health, had spilled cider over it. Oh, how she wept and scolded him. But, thankfully, the stain came out (almost) with the help of a little salt and vinegar, so no great harm was done.

It was Anne who had instilled in him an appreciation of poetry and a deep love of nature and even encouraged him to slide down the Malvern Hills – on a tea tray. He would never forget the exhilaration of gathering speed over the flattened grasses, his fists locked around the handles, then rolling off just before the incline plummeted into what seemed to be the sky and coming up with stalks in his hair, wanting more. Always more.

His parents had also been responsible for his very first composition, for it was at their suggestion that he wrote incidental music for a play called *The Wand of Youth* to be performed by his siblings in the back garden. It had been a great success. Luckily he still had the original manuscripts stacked away in a big trunk in the attic. There were some little gems there, scored at the time for a variety of makeshift instruments – from a double bass made from an old tea chest and a broom handle, to cymbals improvised on a pair of saucepan lids. He'd have to dig out the score and take another look at it – see if there was anything fit to upgrade and re-orchestrate.

Good idea. Make a fresh start at his elegant new home in Hereford, with its big, airy music room giving on to a spacious balcony overlooking the well-groomed lawn. Yes, he'd make a fresh start; pay more attention to Carice and Alice. Start dropping the old friends and acquaintances who gobbled up so much of his time and were frankly beginning to outstay their welcome. The old inspirations had served their purpose.

In any case, there was a new muse on the horizon, one who promised to eclipse all the others, if his pulse were any judge – even Helen Weaver, who was now a fading memory with a family of her own in New Zealand. No, as he cycled westward towards his old home nestling in the hills of Malvern an exquisite musical phrase teased from a solo violin raised his wavering spirits – and the tune it sang was 'Windflower'.

FOURTEEN

Nobilemente

*T*HE ELGARS HAD barely moved into Plas Gwyn before it was time to return to London to be formally knighted by His Majesty the King. The memorable date was 5 July 1904.

He would never forget that moment at the investiture, as in court dress he walked solemnly towards the King awaiting with the sword of honour. Like a gift from an unseen source, a theme at once noble and affirmative and free of bombast had unexpectedly entered his mind to measure the paces. There were seventeen of them, seventeen steps that seemed to atone for all the years of struggle and humiliation and cause them to fade into oblivion. At last he was somebody. That private theme, along with the public tap on the shoulder, confirmed it.

He was to remember that moment, that theme, long after he had completed reworking the Wand of Youth Suite in his music room in Hereford; long after he'd completed his last biblical oratorio, *The Kingdom* (old habits die hard). He remembered it while he hobnobbed with *cognoscenti* and aristocracy alike. It signalled that he had fully justified Alice's faith in him (sorry – Lady Alice, as she was now addressed). It also meant that at last he felt confident enough to tackle the stuff of music that separates the men from the boys – the symphony.

What is a symphony? Arithmetic set to musical notation or an insight into a man's soul? A bit of both perhaps.

The Symphony No. 1 in A flat was launched on the strength of that investiture and the new horizons opening up before him – such as he saw on that breezy sunny day in the summer of 1905, when he first beheld the HMS *Surprise*, dressed overall, riding majestically at anchor at Spithead. What a sense of pride had thrilled his being as he stepped from the plunging cutter on to the gangplank and was piped aboard to the cheers of the entire crew. Then cocktails with the Captain, 'anchors aweigh' and a mini-review of the fleet, as they sailed around the Isle of Wight on the first day of a Mediterranean cruise on which he had been invited by the Admiral of the Fleet, along with his new rich philanthropist chum Frank Schuster.

And there was Ventnor on the starboard beam. How many years ago was the honeymoon? Sixteen? And he was not yet fifty, and it was a sure bet they would be playing his music on the municipal bandstand as the ship sailed past in full regalia. And still nine years to go before their silver wedding anniversary – the date Alice had predicted would see them returning to celebrate twenty-five years of marriage and be greeted at that very spot by a concert of his music. He'd outstripped the prediction by nearly a decade! To think he could ever have doubted it.

Days of sun and indolence, receptions and banquets followed, on that implacable ironclad proclaiming to Elgar and the world that Britannia indisputably rules the waves. And when a company of marines from the ship escorted Sir Edward and a group of VIPs through the hostile streets of Istanbul to a reception given by the British Ambassador the imperious spirit of the troops was sent swaggering through the second movement of the symphony, to show infidels and foes of Great Britain who's Boss.

'Play it like something you hear down by the river,' Elgar once said to an orchestra while rehearsing the sublime slow movement. Most people interpret this as meaning like listening to the wind in the reeds and kindred aspects of nature absorbed on the banks of Teme and Wye. But is it not also possible that the relative failure of his latest choral work *The Kingdom* might have caused Elgar to sublimate his religious visions into songs without words? Is it not just as likely that the serenity occasioned by meditation down by the river, with its blue reflections of sky and cloud, might have metamorphosed into the traditional Catholic image of the Holy Mother, whom Elgar held in high regard? Perhaps it was She whispering to him? And, glancing over his shoulder at those mystical hills, who is to say that the Son of Man was not palpably present for him, during those passing years from boyhood to manhood? Why not? Just think of Blake.

And what is the last movement if not a celebration? Elgar knew that he had written the greatest English symphony of all time and so it proved, receiving close on a hundred performances during the first year of its composition. After an age of emasculated symphonies by the likes of Standford and Parry, here at last was an English symphony by a composer with balls and proud of it. Some symphonies have titles – the 'Fantastic', the 'Surprise', the 'Tragic', etc. Some say Elgar's First should have been called 'The Miracle'.

Unfortunately Haydn beat him to it.

FIFTEEN

Five Stars

EANWHILE 'WINDFLOWER' HAD been waiting in the wings ready to make her entrance. And she did so triumphantly on 10 November 1910, when she appeared to a packed house at the Queen's Hall in London, with Elgar conducting the first performance of his Concerto for Violin and Orchestra in B minor. At the head of the score is the following dedication: '*Aqui está encerrada el alma de ******', which translates as 'Herein is enshrined the soul of *****'.

Five stars, you will notice – as opposed to the mysterious lady of the 'Enigma' Variations, who was only valued at three. But unlike her predecessors, it seems she managed to go through life avoiding the cruel, invasive eye of the camera, even though she was captured in paint by the illustrious brush of her father, Sir John Everett Millais, arguably the greatest of all the Pre-Raphaelite masters. His portraits of the feminine ideal are deservedly legendary, which makes it all the more surprising that he had made his daughter look so mundane and uninspiring, until one realizes that Elgar had much the same attitude to his own daughter, Carice. Perhaps it was a Victorian matter of good taste to overlook a daughter's charms.

But what Dad had failed so dismally to achieve on canvas Edward Elgar brought off with flying colours in music – he idealized her, he immortalized her. She was his Belle Dame Sans Merci. She had him by the balls of inspiration. They first met at a retrospective exhibition of her father's work at Hampton Court. Her name was Alice Stuart-Wortley. Alice Elgar was also present at the event, as was Mr Stuart-Wortley.

So was Frank Schuster, one of Elgar's smart new friends who had recently taken the composer under his wing and may well have played Cupid on more than one occasion. Remember, it was he who had organized that grand cruise of the Mediterranean and later invited Elgar on a motoring tour of Cornwall, where there was yet another *liaison dangereuse* between Edward and his current muse.

What happened at that first encounter remains somewhat of a mystery, though it appears that after the exhibition there was a picnic in the gardens, during which a considerable amount of champagne was consumed, after which Schuster's guests somewhat foolhardily played hide-and-seek in the notorious Hampton Court maze. Which was all great fun, until the euphoria induced by the bubbles and the novelty of being lost in a labyrinth of endless hedgerows began to wear off; when conviviality gave way to taciturnity.

And as the revellers staggered from the exit in dribs and drabs they all began to shiver in the twilight.

'All out, all out,' shouted a park keeper from the top of a folding ladder come lighting-up time.

And Alice watched anxiously as he directed the stragglers to the exit and braced herself for a confrontation with the last two members of the party yet to emerge. She heard their approaching laughter (or so she thought) and did her best not to look censorious. But it wasn't Edu and Mrs Stuart-Wortley who emerged in boisterous spirits but a sailor and his ladyfriend.

'One moment, my man,' said Alice to the park keeper, who was about to fold his ladder and make off. 'Two members of our party are still unaccounted for.'

'Beg pardon, but you are mistaken, madam,' he said, respectfully touching his cap. 'The maze is empty.'

'I find that difficult to believe,' said Alice hotly.

'May I enquire as to their gender, madam?' retorted the park keeper.

'What are you talking about?' demanded the irate Alice. 'What possible difference can it make?'

'With respect, madam, quite a considerable difference,' he replied.

'Very well, if you must know, it was a lady and a gentleman,' snapped Alice.

'Thank you, madam. That's just what I thought.'

A short silence followed – as the park keeper scrutinized the tortured shrubbery yet again before putting into words what more than one member of the party was already thinking. 'Well, they could be lyin' down, of course. And it wouldn't be the first time,' he added with a wicked grin and a wink to Alice, who only managed to hide her outrage by a superhuman effort.

'Perhaps you'd better take a quick look, my man,' said Windflower's husband, fishing in his pocket for a shilling.

'I'm sure that won't be necessary,' said Alice, suddenly fearful of the consequences.

'I suppose the lady could have fainted,' said the park keeper helpfully.

'Yes, and Ted could be administering the kiss of life – I think we're all getting a little fanciful,' cut in Frank Schuster in an effort to restore sanity. 'Let's go home. I'm sure there's a perfectly logical explanation.'

'Some folks gets frustrated and forces their way through the 'edge,' said the park keeper, folding up his ladder. 'Now I must ask you to leave, ladies and gentlemen. I shall be locking up the gates in five minutes' time, thank you. And if they are 'ere 'idin' for a bit of a lark, they're going to have to cuddle up close till mornin', 'coz there's goin' t' be a bit of a frost tonight, mark my words. Goodnight, all.'

And it's a good job he didn't wait for a reply, because he didn't get one – the party was far too busy with their own thoughts.

The sombre mood continued over dinner at Frank's luxurious mansion on the Thames at Bray. Theories as to their disappearance ranged from amnesia to foul play and had Alice wanting to phone the police every five minutes or so. But thankfully she was talked out of such drastic action by their host, who attempted to bring a little levity to the situation.

'Well, if you ask me,' he began innocently enough, 'I reckon they've booked into a discreet little hotel in Hampton Court and . . .' He paused to take in the look of horrified anticipation written large on Alice's countenance. He enjoyed baiting her did Frank, knowing full well that she despised his new money as much as she did his taste in music (Stravinsky) and art (the vorticists). Having savoured the moment, he continued, 'I'm sure they're simply enjoying heavy intercourse of an artistic nature over a slap-up meal.'

'I can just see Edu tearing his way through that hedge with all the vigour of Livingstone in the jungle,' said Alice, gamely rising to the occasion. 'You should have seen him at Birchwood, hacking a path through the undergrowth.'

'And when it comes to a discussion on music,' enthused the truant lady's husband, who happened to be a conservative MP, 'my Alice can go at it hammer and tongs.'

How vulgar, Lady Alice thought to herself as she returned his smile.

But behind that smile was hidden deep concern. After all, Windflower came from a racy set of Bohemian artists – hadn't her father run off with his best friend's wife? Everyone present knew about it, and maybe that knowledge was behind the general reluctance to call in the constabulary.

By the time the truant couple stepped from a hansom at midnight, full of flippant innuendo, Alice was in a state of repressed hysteria. Similar occurrences with Edu and his two cycling sirens came forcibly to mind. Would it never end, this ceaseless philandering?

Poor woman! At sixty she was really beginning to feel her age, though when she looked in a mirror – not something she made a habit of – a woman of seventy stared back at her, pot-bellied, flat-chested, legs like sticks, scrawny arms, slack arse and grey wispy hair. And to make matters worse, there was young Carice always hanging around, to remind her that she had never been anything more than a pallid, anaemic, sexless excuse for a woman.

But she loved Edu without reservation. She could deny him nothing. And if he needed more nubile flesh to feed his inspiration so be it. She would encourage his cannibalistic tendencies, whatever the cost.

That night she offered him no word of reproach as she undressed in the dark and submitted to his demands for anal sex. Was this his way of punishing her for being old and ugly and all dried up?

Well, not quite dried up. Those silent tears were wet enough.

SIXTEEN

Undesirable Aliens

*I*HEARD HIM SAY it. I actually heard him say it. 'When you get to heaven, you'll have a tale to tell that'll make the angels' hair stand on end; won't you, Flash, my boy.'

Of course, he was being facetious, as most people are who talk down to us domestic animals. Children excepted, that is. They know differently. But grown-ups? They just don't think.

If they did, they'd know we pick up on things as fast as a new-born baby – faster – in fact, seven times faster, because if we age at seven times the speed of humans it stands to reason that we assimilate things seven times faster. Anyway, that's enough of that. I think you'll agree I've made my point.

He's a friendly old dog and answers to the name of Sir Edward. He came here to stay early in May. My folks had to go off for a while and said he could have the run of the estate while they were away. His mate came, too. Her name is Alice, and she hates us dogs. Smelly creatures, she calls us. She's a fine one to talk – poor you, should you ever get downwind of her. Bitch.

Anyway, it seems she'd rather put up with me than the German bombs in London. Germans and London I know about; of bombs I know nothing. My master, Rear-Admiral St John Seaforth, is always barking on about the Germans and wanting to kill as many as possible. Killing I also know about. Just ask any rabbit you might bump into around here – if you can find one. Sir Edward also knows about rabbits and often catches sight of them before I do.

He knows about other creatures, too. I caught him talking to a hedgehog once, and the very next day, damned if he didn't carry a saucer of milk all the way from the house to the very spot he'd come across it. And how pleased he was next day when he found it all gone.

'I thought young Spiky would enjoy that little concoction,' he told me. 'I came across the recipe in Germany, of all places. The secret, Flash, is to add a teaspoon of syrup to the milk and mix vigorously. They won't touch it otherwise.'

I nodded my head at this, as it explained why I found it so sweet when I lapped it up when he wasn't watching. Perhaps I looked guilty, because he turned to me with a frown.

'Now, Flash, the time has come for you and I to have a serious talk. It's come to my attention that whenever the words "German" or "Germany" are mentioned you give a little growl. And, truth to tell, most people in this country would react just the same – it's the sign of a true patriot, d'you see? But most people wouldn't believe you. They wouldn't be fooled and they'd demand that you be put behind bars and locked up. Some would even say you should be shot. So, in a way, it's a pity you weren't born a British bulldog instead of an Alsatian or, as some people would say, a German shepherd. Oh, I know you've been taught to stand to attention whenever they play "God Save the King" and all that, but did you ever wonder why they changed your name from Fritz to Flash when war was declared? And I know that's what happened, because the old gardener told me.'

So that's why the old gardener turned against me, I thought. And he used to be so friendly, too, always giving me scraps and such like.

'But whatever the man in the street may think, Fritz, I know that if a marauding Hun in field grey should enter this wood with fixed bayonet bent on doing me harm you'd defend me to the death; and that if any German friend of mine should come down here to take a stroll and chew the fat you'd be the first to lick his hand, even before he'd had a chance to shake mine.

'For truth to tell, Fritz, most of my best friends are of German origin – cultured men and women who wouldn't harm a fly. Musicians, conductors, composers, whose only crime was to wage war against ignorance and indifference and fight to bring the joy of music to this artistically arid land of ours. And now all these good souls – and this includes you, too, Fritz – are the enemy. Suddenly I'm expected, after years and years of friendship, to turn on them and wipe them from the face of the earth. Good people, who championed me and my work at the very time my fellow countrymen were treating me with contempt and trashing me and my music. If it wasn't for the vision of the so-called beastly Hun I'd be languishing in obscurity, still teaching idiots to murder the violin.

'To tell you the truth, Fritz, I'd probably have done away with myself by now. I often contemplated suicide, I promise you.

'Now I'm alone. I've lost them all, all those that were nearest and dearest to me, Fritz. I'd confide in Alice, but she's the truest patriot of them all. She wouldn't understand. But I'm sure you'd understand, if you could, Fritz.

'But you're lucky. You're just a dumb animal, blissfully unaware of the folly of man. There are times when I envy you. I really do.'

And here he bent down and buried his head in the fur around my neck. Silly old thing, I thought, as his tears soaked it. Of course I understand. We're kindred spirits, aren't we?

Flash (alias Fritz) was destroyed shortly after Elgar's departure.

'It was in the post office – on the notice board:

> 'Wanted, odd job man, for general
> Maintenance and light duties around
> Property, including game keeping.
> Apply in person to "Carice"
> c/o Brinkwells Cottage.

'I knew the place well, done odd jobs there for years for the Hubbards, then just for old Mother Hubbard, as we called 'er after 'er old man up and kicked the bucket. She didn't last long after 'e'd gone – couple of months at most. I knocked on the door one Monday morning for me wages as per usual, and I thought she was a long time coming and the dog were barking like buggery. 'Ello, I thought, and put my shoulder to the door and that was that. You'll never guess what a state the place was like, and you'd never believe how I found her.'

'I'm sure I wouldn't, Mr Kitcher, but as I have a train to catch, I'm afraid we'll have to confine ourselves to the people who snapped up the lease. And I take it you called at the cottage and applied for the job?'

'That's right,' Mr Kitcher replied, pausing to take another swig of his pint and sizing up the stranger paying for the round. Instinctively, he distrusted this smiling little lizard of a man, despite the prospects of getting something out of him.

As for his part, the stranger leaning against the bar of the Dog and Duck, supping a large scotch and facing a short, stocky sort of man with a head that put him in mind of a beetroot, simply kept smiling and said, 'Can I get you a chaser, Mr Kitcher?'

'You tryin' to get I drunk?' the wily Kitcher enquired.

'Not at all,' replied the stranger, whose name was Miles Spooner. 'You were just going to tell me about your interview with Miss Carice.'

'Was I now? Well, let me see. Yes. Plain little thing, very solemn-like. Never seen 'er smile in – how long is it now? Must be nigh on three years. The old woman's much the same, very strait-laced, only speak when you're spoken to and always reply "Your Ladyship". Yes, Your Ladyship, no, Your Ladyship, may I kiss yer arse, Yer Ladyship? I soon learned 'ow to 'andle 'er. Used to allow me the privilege to pick blackberries with 'er. " Wash yer 'ands first, if you please, Kitcher" – never ever asked me first name, same with the maid. Always Barton. Do this, Barton. Do that. Never Jenny, never once . . .'

'So did you wash your hands before blackberrying with Her Ladyship, Mr Kitcher?' queried Spooner.

'No, I did not,' replied Mr Kitcher with a coarse guffaw, 'though you won't want to print this, I betcha. I pissed on the buggers instead.'

Spooner simply smiled and thought: He's not as stupid as he looks, and he's right, I can't print it – more's the pity.

'How about Sir Edward. Did you see much of him?'

'Old fartarse, you mean. Fine, we 'ad a lot in common, 'im and me.'

'Don't tell me. Let me guess,' said Spooner, beginning to tire of the man's attitude. 'A mutual love of Mozart, was it?'

''Oo's 'e when 'e's at 'ome? I was referrin' to the gee-gees.'

'Horses, you mean? Gymkhanas and that sort of thing . . . Did you used to attend them together?'

'Did we, 'ell! I was referrin' to the races. I pretty well learned 'im all 'e knows about bettin'. Odds on, ten to one, each way – it was a foreign language to 'im to start with. But 'e soon picked it up, and once 'e got the 'ang of it, 'e'd be up for a flutter whenever 'e knew I was off to the bettin' shop. We'd go over the *Sportin' Life* together as soon as I picked it up from the post office every Monday. "Mum's the word," 'e said on more than one occasion. "This is our little secret, Kitcher," 'e used to say. "Not a word to Her Ladyship, now, she wouldn't understand, bless 'er little 'eart." And that wasn't the only little secret we 'ad between us, believe you me. There were others a-plenty.'

'Such as . . . ?' prompted Spooner.

'Such as would be worth more 'n a pint a' bitter an' a packet a' crisps, mate, I can assure you. But I can tell you this. 'E 'ad a real feelin' for the outdoor life. The old lady was always findin' excuses for poppin' up to London; so did young Carice, come to that. Anyway, she 'ad a part-time job in a 'ospital – teachin' officers blinded by mustard gas, basket work or weavin' or some such when all they really wanted to do was give 'er a good gropin'; least that's what I would 'ave done. Would 'ave done 'er a power a' good, too, I reckon, 'coz there was one randy virgin if ever I saw one.'

'And how did Elgar spend his days?' asked Spooner.

''E liked nothin' better than sawin' down saplin's and makin' a big bonfire a' the buggers. Thought 'e was doin' 'is bit for the war effort or summit. Mad, if you ask me, but 'armless with it all the same. 'E wouldn't 'arm a fly, nor an ant neither. There was a big ant 'eap right outside 'is studio. I was all for doin' away with it, but 'e wouldn't 'ear of it. Used to watch it for 'ours. Fed the birds, too, and the hedgehogs. Used to set down saucers of milk for 'em. Barmy, if you ask me, but 'armless enough.'

'Tell me about the studio. What went on in there?' said Spooner.

'Oh, wouldn't you like to know,' said Kitcher with a crafty chuckle. 'It was well away from the 'ouse and 'idden by trees. It 'ad a big piano in it and a sort a' couch.'

'What do you mean, a sort of couch? Do you mean a divan or daybed, perhaps?'

Kitcher sized Spooner up suspiciously. 'I said it was a sort a' couch,' he said steadfastly, 'and that is what it was.'

'And did he often play?'

'Not 'alf,' said Kitcher with a wink. 'Specially when the ladies was present.'

'It's no secret Elgar has dozens of female admirers . . . of his music,' said Spooner, airing his knowledge. 'Rosa Burley, Alice Stuart-Wortley, Dora Penny, Lady Mary Lygon, to name but a few.'

'And a good few more besides, on the quiet,' said Kitcher, going one (or two) better. 'Even 'ad a Kraut bitch down 'ere once. Bleedin' Mata Hari if you asked me. Bugger me if 'Er Ladyship didn't join 'em and they were all at it. Barkin' away in German fit to bust. What do you make of that?'

'What did you make of it?'

'I done what you or any true patriot would've done. I went straight to the police.'

'And found you'd made a terrible mistake. Your Mata Hari turned out to be a naturalized alien who has appeared in concert with Sir Edward reciting "Le Drapeau Belge" by the Belgian poet Cammaerts, which Elgar set to music,' said Spooner, warming to the fray, 'and got your name in the papers and also got you fired.'

'And got you on the first train down 'ere.'

'To make you a reasonable offer for an article called "Fond Memories of a Famous English Gentleman", but if you're not interested we can just forget it.'

'Top 'er up, mate,' said Kitcher, nodding at his empty glass, 'an' I'll think about it.'

A few pints further on they struck a deal, but the shocking article was never published – the editor considered it libellous. Poor Spooner!

SEVENTEEN

Requiem

*E*LGAR, SLUMPED ON a splendid throne that had once been the seat of power for an exalted Hindu panjandrum, seemed nothing more than a shabby usurper. There had been a time when it could have been Sir Edward's natural habitat, but with Alice gone all the old pomp and circumstance seemed to have gone with her, including all his decorations and the sword of honour he had dumped in her coffin.

He looked about the spacious studio, deserted now except for the throne on which he was sitting and a billiard-table covered in a white sheet, in front of the floor-to-ceiling window which gave on to a view of scaffolding where once had stood a row of poplars. The neighbour had cut them down without warning while Elgar was spending summer in the cottage at Brinkwells, which he had also been forced to vacate for a different reason – failure to secure an extension of the lease.

Here in London it was simply a question of money; or, rather, the lack of it. Things were tight. He had just received a cheque from his publishers for a little over five hundred pounds – the grand total of his share of royalties over the last five years. Pathetic!

Truth to tell, hadn't things been for ever thus. Alice had to go to court in order to break a trust to provide funds for the purchase of this white elephant, and hadn't friends rallied around and pretty well furnished the entire place *gratis*?

And a very fine place Severn House had been – situated in stylish Hampstead and especially designed for the grandiose taste of a fashionable Victorian painter; thus equally fitting, according to some critics, for Sir Edward Posh and his snooty Lady . . . particularly for the snooty lady, who after years of voluntary (if reluctant) exile had, with Edu's sudden elevation, claimed the metropolitan status to which she had always aspired.

And now that she was gone, so was the need for the Emperor's New Home regardless of cost.

Noise outside at the bottom of the garden, noise inside with the removal men continually up and down the stairs. Soon they would be knocking on the door to strip the room of both the billiard-table and the silly souvenir on which he was sitting. One of the removal men was whistling 'Land of Hope and Glory' by unhappy coincidence.

'Shut up that row,' roared Elgar, but the man didn't hear him and kept on whistling. God, how he hated that tune. He put his hands over his ears to shut it out.

But he couldn't shut out the images that went with it – images of countless wounded men marching through dirty yellow fog into a vast open grave, into which they stumbled and tumbled. The blind, the maimed, the shell-shocked, the mad, the disembowelled, the faceless, the fearful, the poor agonized sods with shattered bones, bleeding lungs and gangrened tongues – gasping for air as the rancid bile gurgled in their throats, distorting the words rising from every living corpse as they slipped and skidded down a cascade of mud and gore on to the rotting bodies of the fallen, still struggling to give voice to their own Requiem with their very last breath: 'Death of Hope and Glory'.

A brief knock caused him to swing around in his chair as someone entered the room, unbidden. It was his old friend Rosa Burley – momentarily shocked into silence by the sight of Elgar in tears, which continued to flow unabated.

She'd never seen him cry before – in all the thirty years she'd known him. He'd had cause a-plenty, ranging from unwarranted discrimination to the disintegration of his ordered world, culminating in the death of his wife. And throughout all those stressful years, Rosa surmised, the pressure had been building. His stoicism had finally collapsed in a torrent of grief.

May it bring him a measure of relief, she thought.

Feeling guilty for having intruded on an intensely private moment, she continued none the less with the business at hand, softening her tone as best she could. 'The men have almost finished,' she said. 'They'll be down in a few minutes to dismantle the billiard-table – if that's all right?'

'That's all right,' he said in a choked voice and turned away, searching in his jacket pockets for a handkerchief.

As she closed the door quietly behind her she heard him blow his nose.

Poor old soul – finished, all washed up. That was the general consensus. Were they right? With the old lady gone, the driving force that had continually spurred him on had also gone . . . temporarily, Rosa liked to think.

An hour later the slam of the front door sounded the death of an era and had barely echoed into the past before Rosa turned to Elgar with a big smile to announce the birth of a new one – or so she hoped.

'Now, at last we can make it official,' she beamed.

And so ended a beautiful friendship.

Call it bad timing. The idea that any woman could ever replace Alice was absolutely, violently abhorrent to Elgar.

In vain, Rosa pointed out that she had been as much a mother to Carice as Her Ladyship; even more so, perhaps. Hadn't she taken the child off their hands during the holidays for year after year to give them a break? Hadn't she advised Elgar on every aspect of his career in general and composition in particular? Hadn't she been his constant companion in their exploration of the highways and byways of his beloved Worcestershire? Not to mention their more intimate moments?

All this Elgar readily admitted to himself but would gladly forgo all the obvious advantages of such a union rather than allow a commoner to step into Her Ladyship's sacred shoes. The very idea of deposing her for a lesser being was positively sacrilegious.

Elgar was vitriolic in his rejection of Rosa's proposal. 'You must be joking,' he said coldly. 'You're half the woman she is.'

But Rosa had her revenge: by sending the outraged composer several secret journals Alice had kept over the years and which had come to light during the eviction from Severn House – which Rosa had thoughtfully supervised.

If things had gone according to her wishes Elgar would never have set eyes on them; in fact, Rosa might well have destroyed them. But as it was, he received them by registered post one day shortly after the row – a day that cast a long shadow over the remainder of his life.

There was no note of explanation enclosed in the parcel, simply three small leather-bound ledgers that were completely unfamiliar to Elgar. On opening the first book, he recognized the handwriting instantly as that of Alice. It was a diary, with each entry preceded by a date.

He started to read.

APRIL 16, 1910

The memory of those sublime moments spent together during our time at Tintagel have blossomed into a ravishing melody in the slow movement of my new concerto which I shall christen the 'Windflower' theme.

MAY 6, 1910

Invited W.H. Reid to come down with his fiddle and run through the concerto. When he came to the 'Windflower' theme he insisted on playing through it twice. 'I've fallen head over heels in love with that melody,' he enthused. 'Pure inspiration.'

My sentiments exactly, I thought to myself.

'And I know who we have to thank for that,' he said, winking at simpering Alice . . . If only they knew the truth.

NOVEMBER 11, 1910

Desolate, dearest Windflower that you were unable to be present last night in the Queen's Hall to hear for yourself the consummation of our love brought to life by Kreisler. Even so I know you were there in spirit fused with mine alone.

Alice, poor soul, insists on calling it 'our' concerto.

A chill gripped Elgar's heart like a hand from the grave, as he strove to fight off the fearful implications forming in his mind. He put down the book, picked up another, opened it at random and read:

SEPTEMBER 16, 1916

Dear Lalla,

The memory of our time in the woods together here at Brinkwells last week is a cherished memory that has flowered into the love theme in my new quartet which heralds a new direction in my art for which you and you alone are entirely responsible.

Write and let me know when you can come again, preferably when Alice is up in town on the 23rd, 24th, 25th.

Eternal love, E.

Elgar dropped the book as if he'd been burned. And in a sense he had, for even as a lapsed Catholic he was still a firm believer in hell, and that's where he had consigned himself until death would momentarily reprieve him.

It was clear as day. These three volumes were a catalogue of sins he had committed against Alice throughout his entire married life. The tributes that were her due he had conferred on others – a succession of fantasy lovers, most of whom were happily married. Love letters he had cynically given to her to dispatch along with bills and business letters she had faithfully posted nearly every day of their marriage. And it had never occurred to him that she might have steamed them open to steal a kind word or a declaration he had long denied her.

And still she had stuck by him, though each missive was like a stab wound to her soul. Elgar was, at heart, a sensitive man. He got the message.

It crushed him for ever.

EIGHTEEN

The Pilgrimage

*W*AS HE REALLY up to making the journey alone? Carice thought not. She wouldn't offer to accompany him herself, it's true, but there was no reason why he shouldn't take his valet – or one of his old girlfriends, come to that. Rosa Burley would surely jump at the chance, no matter how long the interval since her father and Rosa had last seen each other – in the past they had often gone mountaineering in Germany together. Or that awful actress Lalla Vanderveldt. Hadn't they gone to the lakes on holiday together way back in the war?

'We were all there,' Elgar elucidated. 'We stayed at that splendid little hotel at Ullswater: me, your mother, Lalla and both her parents.'

'Must be all of ten years ago,' said Carice. 'How time flies. Anyway, why this sudden desire to revisit the Lake District when you've got the Malvern Hills on your doorstep?'

'I have my reasons. I have my reasons,' Elgar murmured mysteriously.

'On no, Father, not another Enigma, please,' remonstrated Carice.

'Got it in one!' said Elgar with a smile.

'Is she blonde or brunette?'

'What makes you think it's a she?'

'I suppose it's another dog, then,' said Carice with a mock groan. 'I hope it's a St Bernard, then it could pull you all the way up and provide you with a drink on the summit. Does this mystery peak you hope to conquer have a name?'

'It's called Great Gable,' said Elgar. 'And it's rather special.'

'Then you must tell me about it some time,' said Carice. 'But now I must go; and if you'll take my advice you'll forget this mountaineering nonsense and settle for a few relaxing days in Bournemouth. I hear Dan Godfrey's conducting an all "you" programme there at the weekend. Bye!' And she was gone.

Thank God, thought Elgar.

In the event, Elgar did take his valet – as far as the base camp, as it were.

On the first leg of their journey they boarded a train at Euston Station at eight- thirty in the morning on 11 July 1926, Elgar travelling first-class 'smoking' and his man, Harry Jeffries, in second-class 'non-smoking'. And every hour on the hour Harry would enquire as to his master's needs and at noon produced a picnic hamper from which he served a light lunch of quails' eggs and Belgian pâté washed down with a half-bottle of Dom Perignon and finished off with a slice of Stilton and a glass of vintage port. By this time they were chuffing into Penrith, three hundred miles to the north, where their connection was waiting at an adjacent platform.

Thirty minutes later they were on the station forecourt in the little town of Keswick, organizing a pony and trap to take them to the Lodore Falls Hotel at the head of Borrowdale Valley. Soon they were clip-clopping along the lakeside road, Elgar and his man suffering in silence while the local driver treated the tourists to a mine of useless information. They were both much relieved when the roar of the falls drowned him out, announcing their arrival at the hotel.

Soon after, bathed and refreshed, Elgar was able to light his pipe and relax into an armchair by the bedroom window. As he gazed up Derwentwater, he contemplated the magnificent mountain of Skiddaw. Rising provocatively above the little town of Keswick on the northern shores of the 'Queen of the Lakes', Skiddaw was indeed an awesome sight to behold.

'Coleridge was right,' said Elgar aloud to an empty room. 'That mysterious mountain dominating all it surveys like a gigantic, shrouded, almighty, enthroned figure really could be "God made manifest!"'

Suddenly the far-off Malvern Hills came to mind – seductive and voluptuous, putting him in mind of a reclining nude. Both locations were inspirational in their different ways – one sacred, the other profane. And, as Elgar drifted and dreamed, the lights of Keswick began to appear in an effort to rival the stars just now starting to spark in the sky.

Elgar said his prayers and went to bed.

After an early breakfast, prior to which the valet had helped his master into his climbing gear, they waited in the foyer for the appearance of the local man with the pony and trap they had booked the day before. He was late – not very late but late enough to sour Elgar's mood a little. The situation did not improve when the man announced without ceremony that 'Great Gable' was off – everything above a thousand feet was fog bound.

Cursing, Elgar strode outside and looked in the direction of Skiddaw – gone – lost in the heavy mist rising from the lake. And according to the man – not his favourite person by now – it wasn't expected to lift, either, 'Not this side of noon, anyways.'

The possibility of poor visibility had never occurred to Elgar. For a moment he was stymied.

'If the gentleman is set on a climb, why not try Castle Crag?' suggested their self-appointed guide. 'Just under a thousand feet, with glorious views up the valley. It's quite a favourite with the tourists, especially ladies and the old folk.' (Unwelcome facts that hardened Elgar's heart against it right away.) Other points of interest were 'an abandoned quarry halfway up and a recent memorial to local lads lost in the war'.

Here Elgar perked up. Though he had his heart set on Great Gable, this lesser peak, it seems, was also claiming distinction as a sort of Mecca to the memory of the fallen. In the case of Great Gable, on every Good Friday morning since the start of hostilities, streams of mourners could be seen making their annual pilgrimage up Honister Pass to the summit to pray for their loved ones gone before.

Elgar had discovered the custom ten years earlier when he had paid his own respects for the first time and vowed to repeat them every decade for the rest of his life. True, it was not Good Friday, but to Elgar 12 July held a meaning not unlike the death of the Son of Man. It was the day Elgar's own son had also been sacrificed to save mankind.

When Elgar had read of the boy's death in one of the never-ending casualty lists in the London *Times* that terrible July morning in 1916 at Brinkwells he felt something snap loose in him, like a too taut string. He was plunged into a sickly nothingness. His one dominant thought had been to get away from the place where part of him had also died. And, to make matters worse, there was no one to share his pain.

At the time Alice had attributed his distress to overwork, the war, powdered milk, hay fever – anything and everything. But at least she got one thing right – his need to get away. Quite naturally, her first suggestion was a trip to the

Malvern Hills; they invariably raised his spirits just as soon as he caught sight of them.

'No!' he bellowed. He was 'heartily sick of the Malverns – mere molehills!' What he didn't tell her was that they reminded him of the dead boy's mother, Helen Weaver, the one with whom he had shared them since childhood, while Alice was still a spoilt memsahib in Bengal.

Well, what about a week or so at Severn House in Hampstead? They could take in a few shows, entertain friends to dinner . . .

'Too hot,' he retorted. 'All that beastly black-out, you can't breathe. Stifling . . .'

The real reason he kept to himself. It was fear of reawakening old memories of a boy lying on a bed of pain in the local hospital where he had been sent after being wounded on the Western Front.

He had learned of the boy's whereabouts from Helen's brother, now resident in Cornwall and with whom he had sporadically kept in touch over the years. What a wrench it had been when the lad had been patched up and sent back to France. No, he couldn't go back to Hampstead.

Then, almost at her wit's end, Alice suggested the Lake District.

Why not? Especially when she promised to coax along Lalla Vanderveldt, a voluptuous actress, to keep him company. And it was Lalla, a committed fell walker, who had informed Elgar those ten years ago about the then recent custom of honouring the war dead with prayers on the summit of Great Gable.

Since a repeat visit today was impossible, he allowed the local to drive him along the valley to the foot of Castle Crag, with instructions to return in a couple of hours, along with the valet and some light refreshment. The climb would be a bit of a sweat but nothing compared with the rocky path to the top of Great Gable. Perhaps the fog had been a blessing in disguise. What if it had proved too much for him? What if he'd been forced to turn back? Ten years of indulgence had taken their toll.

So he took frequent rests as he ascended, during which he allowed himself to reflect on the real reason why Helen Weaver had suddenly upped and gone to the other side of the world. Yes, religious differences and ill health had been contributing factors; but shame and shame alone had been the major cause for her ultimate departure.

The shame of having a child out of wedlock.

In vain Elgar had promised to make an honest woman of her, but to

Helen's mind that would do little to save her reputation. It was over, blighted for ever. She must lose herself and the child as far away as she could arrange.

Strangely, her fiercely self-protective and irrevocable decision to flee was also made out of consideration for Elgar himself. The ensuing scandal would have put an end to his career as a successful music teacher to the highly respectable maidens of Malvern, without question. Not only would he have been a social outcast he would also have brought disgrace on the rest of the family and probably put his father out of business.

So why didn't he do the honourable thing and go with her to become New Zealand's greatest composer? Silly question!

Before he was quite prepared for it Elgar reached the craggy summit, scattered with fir trees surrounding a natural shrine of rough granite. Within the rock was mounted a polished bronze plaque, on which were inscribed the ninety-odd names of local lads who had left the security of this blessed valley to die in an alien wasteland of unimaginable horror.

He looked beyond the shrine and up the valley towards the Godlike sight of Skiddaw materializing from the morning mist, indifferent to the fact that the boys who had played happily on its slopes would never return to mature in its shadows. Aware but uncaring . . . as is a God's right.

For some reason Elgar thought of the ant hill outside his studio at Brinkwells. Those insects were far closer to God than was man. The ants were part of the fabric of God. They had created their God, made Him out of the material of His universe, lived within Him, became part of Him. The living God of the ants was devotion made manifest, just as Skiddaw mountain was Coleridge's God made manifest.

And now this God was capriciously hiding Himself again in a cloak of invisibility, which even reached as far as Elgar five miles to the south.

The trees surrounding the man on his knees before the altar became mere shapes in the mist, anonymous men lost in a gas attack in no man's land. He was suddenly chilled and started coughing and gasping for breath, blundering about in a desperate search for the sole way down – bumping into trees, crashing along paths that ended in precipitous cul-de-sacs. Finally, in full panic, he passed out.

He awoke to find the driver and the valet bending over him. Between them they helped him down the hill. That same night he was on the sleeper from Carlisle, with an ambulance waiting at Euston to rush him to the London Clinic for an emergency throat operation..

As soon as he could he asked for his wallet. Waiting until the room was empty, he shakily took out a snapshot of a smiling soldier, one who looked considerably younger than the thirty-one years that had elapsed since Helen Weaver had kissed Elgar goodbye.

The idea that Helen may have had a miscarriage and conceived a son by the man she eventually married never entered Elgar's head. He simply did not permit it to do so.

NINETEEN

The Same Coin

*M*Y NAME IS Charles Danvers, and I am a part-time member of the Croydon Philharmonic Orchestra. Actually, most of us are part timers, including Mrs Vera Hockman, with whom I share a desk among the first violins. It's because of her that I found myself on the morning of Sunday 28 May 1933 sitting behind the great Sir Edward Elgar on a de Havilland Dragon at Croydon aerodrome, about to take off on a trip to Paris.

It was a dream come true. I couldn't believe it. And it was all down to Vera Hockman, bless her cotton socks.

'Charles, I want you to do me a favour,' she said to me one night as we were tuning up. 'I want you to accompany Elgar to Paris as his valet.'

Naturally I thought it was a joke, but before I could think of a suitable rejoinder the conductor walked on to the platform and launched us into what turned out to be a rather scrappy performance of Elgar's Cockaigne Overture. Ten minutes later I turned to Vera during the undeserved applause and said, 'I play second fiddle to no man, not even a knight of the realm', which I thought was rather smart of me.

But Vera just grinned and said, 'Join me for a pint in the Crown and Anchor after the concert and I'll give you another chance.' Then she buried her head in the score of the next piece in the programme, and as it was Richard Strauss's Don Juan, an absolute bugger, I did likewise.

Later that evening down at the pub she elaborated on her bizarre request, and despite my initial reservations I eventually accepted her proposal. Apparently the recording company His Master's Voice was financing a promotional concert in Paris, with Elgar conducting a performance of his Violin Concerto. It seems Sir Edward wasn't exactly to the taste of the average Gallic music lover; and Fred Gaisberg, the artistic director of the company, speculated that a personal appearance by our illustrious composer might change their opinions and whet their appetites for more.

'So far so good, but where do I come in, Vera?'

'The old boy needs looking after, and the regular valet is off sick.'

'Then why don't you go?' I said, looking her straight in the eye, for, like everyone else in the band, I was fully aware of their close relationship.

'Because I want to avoid a scandal,' she replied coolly. 'If the press got to know about us they'd have a field day. Anyway, knowing how you admire the old chap, I thought you'd jump at the opportunity.'

'You know my aspirations. I want to be a writer, not a manservant.'

'Which is why I've already contacted the editor of the *Croydon Gazette*. He is willing to pay you twenty guineas for an article entitled "Sir Edward Takes Paris by Storm".'

'And what if he doesn't?'

'Silly question,' she replied, putting me in my place.

'I know nothing about valeting.'

'That's obvious,' said Vera, reaching forward to adjust my bow-tie. 'Don't worry about it. Tomorrow I'll give you a list of everything you need to know; it's child's play – you'll find him as good as gold and you won't have to put your hand in your pocket, either. And, on top of that, you'll get wages – minus my commission, of course.'

For a moment I took her seriously, until she gave me a wink and a wicked grin. I was captivated. She was enchanting. What a lucky old sod. I was almost jealous.

'So you'll do it?' she said, smiling and taking my hand as our knees touched beneath the table. I smiled back, nodding. I could feel myself blushing.

And a little more than a week later here I was taxiing across the tarmac about to take to the skies for the first time in my life. It was a first for Elgar, too.

'I say, young man,' he said over his shoulder, as we bumped along, 'you're not a Catholic by any chance, are you?'

'Why, yes, Sir Edward,' I replied, somewhat startled, 'as a matter of fact, I am.'

'Well, I don't suppose you've brought a rosary along with you . . . ?' he ventured, somewhat tentatively.

Shame-faced, I refrained from mentioning that it was burning a hole in the palm of my hand and simply said, 'Yes.'

'Well, if you're not using it now, I'd like to borrow it for a minute or two,' he muttered, holding up his hand.

Without a word I passed it over the top of the seat so that it brushed his fingers, whereupon he almost snatched it from me and began muttering his prayers – just as we became airborne. It was almost a miracle, or so it seemed at the time.

Then came a chuckle from the occupant in the seat across the aisle from Elgar, a sound that grew into an irreverent guffaw. The guilty party was none other than Fred Gaisberg, the bigwig from HMV who had masterminded the trip.

'My Lord,' he exclaimed,' is this the man whose heart was closed against the Catholic faith for ever and who publicly cursed God because he was against art?'

'Well, I'm getting closer to Him every minute,' said Elgar, as the plane climbed higher and higher in the heavens. 'Perhaps He'll hear my prayers at last,' he thundered before returning to his devotions.

I simply curled up and had to stuff a hand in my mouth to stifle my mirth.

By the time we landed safely at Le Bourget a couple of hours later we were all in good spirits – due in part to Sir Edward's prayers, no doubt; though the two bottles of Dom Perignon we consumed during the flight undoubtedly gave them lift.

I am ashamed to say I missed the performance of the Violin Concerto given that evening at the Salle Pleyel with Sir Edward conducting and Yehudi Menuhin as soloist. Worse still, I failed in my duties to Sir Edward to the extent that instead of looking after him he ended up looking after me.

To be specific, he not only undressed me and put me to bed but popped his head around the door in the morning to see how I was doing.

'I feel badly for letting you down so, Sir Edward,' I stammered. 'It won't happen again, I promise you.'

'From now on, it's nothing stronger than Perrier water for you, my boy,' he said, coming to sit on the bed. 'And don't worry about me. It wasn't the first time I've slept in the buff; and, as you can see, I still remember how to dress myself.'

At this he smiled kindly, and I wondered if I should draw his attention to the fact that he was wearing odd socks. Deciding that discretion was the better part of valour I asked how the concert had gone instead.

'Disgraceful,' he growled. 'An all-English affair sponsored by HMV to boost sales. Good intentions, bad programming. The first item was Façade by that new fellow, what's-his-name, Willie something-or-other.'

'Walton,' I interjected, suspecting that he knew perfectly well.

'"Facile" would be closer to the mark,' he said scornfully. 'All pastiche polkas, foxtrots, tangos and the like; stuff the French do so much better. Do you know Milhaud's Bœuf Sur le Toit? *Très amusant!* . . . Then came Bantock's "Hebridean" Symphony – all sheep bleating and seagulls shrieking. The last place on earth you'd ever want to visit, especially if you were French. Nothing but porridge – morning, noon and night. The first half came to an end with On Hearing the First Cuckoo in Spring. Delius really is perverse – of all the wondrous birdsong in the world to rhapsodize, he has to go and pick the single bird on the planet that can only manage two notes and boring ones at that! Hardly surprising that when it came the turn of my concerto after the interval the hall was half empty. Disastrous!'

Before the irate composer had time to elaborate further a knock came at the door and a maid entered with a steaming bowl of coffee.

'When you're washed and dressed, pack your things and meet me in the foyer,' said Elgar, rising to his feet. 'We're leaving for Grez-sur-Loing in thirty minutes.'

'Grez-sur-Loing?' I said in surprise.

'Grez-sur-Loing!' Elgar repeated, making for the door. 'Little village just south of Paris. We're off to spend the day with Fred.'

Fred? I thought to myself, as Elgar hurried from the room.

Fred Gaisberg from HMV? I wasn't particularly keen to see him again, having overexuberantly embraced the astonished man after making a safe landing the day before. But there he was. I made an attempt to regain my poise by saying very little and peering straight ahead, as though to be the first to spot our mystery destination.

By this time we were bowling along the boulevards in a taxi bound for Grez. It became obvious as the two men chatted that there was yet another Fred to be included in today's outing, one that awaited us on arrival. Could it be a friend of Elgar's or a relative perhaps? I sincerely hoped not. Though my brain was working rather sluggishly I deduced that the Fred in question might quite possibly be Frederick Delius. I knew Delius was living in self-imposed exile in France, though I didn't know exactly where

I fastened on Delius in my imagination and said a cheerful little prayer to the Virgin that it be so. When you consider Elgar's dismissive attitude towards Delius expressed earlier in my room, it might seem odd that I deemed a meeting likely. I certainly thought twice about questioning Elgar regarding this other 'Fred'. But the prospect of seeing my two favourite composers face to face was just too exciting for words.

Spot on! We arrived at Delius's riverside residence just in time for lunch, which I'm guessing was probably according to a prearranged itinerary. Delius, looking pale and gaunt and dressed all in white, received us in the garden. Seated somewhat stiffly in a high-backed chair, he looked more dead than alive.

I knew that he was both blind and paralysed, but I was totally unprepared for this spectre; he had once been an intrepid mountaineer, as well as a handsome composer. His choral masterpiece 'Song of the High Hills' was always buzzing around my head whenever I got the opportunity to go fell-walking – particularly if it was a hot summer day. But if there was a fresh breeze blowing then Elgar's Introduction and Allegro for Strings invariably came to mind.

And here they both were, two of our greatest English composers, meeting for the first time in a French provincial garden – the inspiration for much of Delius's finest works. In a Summer Garden and Summer Night on the River I found to be particularly evocative. In fact, as we sat there surrounded by late flowering roses with the Loire flowing serenely by I couldn't keep the music out of my head.

There were five of us present – myself, Fred Gaisberg, who had set up the meeting, the two composers and Jelka Delius, the invalid's long-suffering wife – who, I gathered, was largely responsible for the earthly paradise around us. After brief introductions all round, champagne was served.

Before accepting a glass I looked at Elgar for approval.

He smiled and waved an index finger, which I took as meaning just one glass. In any event I took one and joined everyone in a toast.

'To English music,' proposed Fred Gaisberg. With a flourish, I raised my glass along with him. We were the only ones to do so.

'English music,' exclaimed Delius with disgust. 'What's that? I've never heard any.'

There was an awkward pause as we wondered how Elgar would take it. I just hoped he didn't see Jelka – who was sitting close – give her husband a nudge.

'Present company excepted,' the great man added, smiling blindly in Elgar's direction.

Elgar was the perfect guest. 'Couldn't agree more, Fred. Ever since Purcell we've been a nation of musical midgets.'

'So let's drink to our two national giants,' I blurted out in desperation. Gaisberg caught my eye and gave me a nod of gratitude before adding his own endorsement; affable fellow – I could almost hug him again.

'To our musical giants,' he roared heartily. The guests clinked glasses, Jelka smiled sweetly and we all drank deeply.

Next came the presentation.

'Fred,' Elgar began, 'not having the good fortune to have a conductor of the stature of Sir Thomas Beecham to promote my work, my good friend Fred Gaisberg here has allowed me to conduct a selection of my repertoire in his recording studio. And will gladly offer the same facility to you, Delius, just as soon as you're back on your feet again.'

'And don't think I won't take you up on that,' said Delius, with a strange laugh. 'And, remember, if my arms are still useless I can always conduct with my dick.'

This shocked me into silence, but, to their credit, the others managed an awkward laugh – after which Elgar picked up the threads of his little speech.

'Anyway, to cut a long story short, Fred, I've brought you a copy of my first symphony.'

'All twelve sides of it,' cut in Gaisberg.

'Don't worry, I'm not going to play you the lot; but I would like you to sample a little of the slow movement. It's what I felt as I sat on the banks of the River Wye one wonderful May morning. My little girl Carice was with me, and I suppose it's really more about her than the surroundings; or maybe it was my reaction to her loving spirit in that moment of time, in that particular place, amid the miracle of creation . . .'

Here he came to an abrupt stop. I think he'd said more than he intended to. I got the feeling that we had just been privy to something that in other circum-stances could only be dragged out of him under torture. Perhaps he wanted to impart something to a composer he felt he should relate to, because of the little they had in common. But with a few exceptions their music was worlds apart.

Or was it? They certainly shared a poetic sensibility, a love of nature and an acute sense of place – not only in nature's realm but also in the capital cities they knew and loved. In Elgar's case this was the Cockaigne Overture – In London Town, while Delius's symphonic poem *Paris* is a dawn-to-dusk evocation of her gay Bohemian life at the turn of the century.

They were also both provincial lads, born within easy reach of the country-side that inspired their art. We know all about Elgar's Malvern Hills' but less, perhaps, about the moors outside Bradford where Delius spent most of his formative years. Like Elgar he also started off working for his dad; in his case, a wealthy industrialist involved in the wool trade.

Then there was their mutual fascination with religion and the important role it played in their art. Elgar the Catholic and Delius the pagan were poles apart theologically – the Bible and the inspiration of Cardinal Newman on the one hand, Nietzsche and Zarathustra on the other. From the ridiculous to the sublime, you might say – or vice-versa, depending on your point of view. Either way, both men were responsible for some great religious music, from Elgar's Gerontius to Delius's Mass of Life.

They also shared a love of Germany and its culture. Delius even studied there. And it was a well-known fact that neither had been accepted by the British musical establishment and that both had been forced into exile – Elgar in his own land, Delius in France. And who knows that, but for the indefatigable fortitude of his deceased wife Alice, Elgar might have suffered a similar fate to Delius, enduring indefinitely his native land's indifference.

Jelka was not like the late Lady Elgar. I could tell she was a gentle soul, a consummate artist and, despite that covert nudge, not in the least pushy.

Perhaps the only thing the two women had in common was the blind eye they turned to their husbands' philandering. If I knew about it, you could hardly suppose that they didn't.

'Jelka, get the servants to bring out the gramophone,' said Delius. 'The young man here might like to give them a hand. Let's see if we can evoke the conditions that so inspired Sir Edward – though I'm afraid we will have to forgo the young lady. We were never blessed with children . . .' – and here he gave a wicked chuckle – 'well, none I'll admit to, anyway.'

And once again there was a feeling of unease in the air, which I gratefully left behind as I followed Jelka into the house to help with the gramophone. This accomplished, the manservant slung Delius over his shoulder like a sack of potatoes and carried him down to the water's edge where the maid had planted the chair. Then, as Jelka refilled our glasses (I felt it rude to refuse),

Elgar (fortunately, with his back to us) wound up the gramophone and put on a record.

We listened in various attitudes as the music combined with the buzz of bees and a variety of trilling birdsong. Gaisberg and I lounged on the grass, the servants stood like statues on either side of Delius, who sat stiff as a ramrod, while Jelka sat on a stool with her knitting. Meanwhile Elgar himself leaned against the gramophone cabinet with his eyes tight shut – trying his best to shut out his surroundings, I suspect.

And so four rather painful minutes passed by as everyone strained to relax. Swish, swish and Elgar was lifting the lid to play the next side, one down, two to go, I thought – as the needle zwipped into the groove and the music started to flow once more.

I looked at Delius with his closed hooded eyes and wondered what he was thinking. Then it occurred to me that he might be asleep. By now the servants were shifting from one foot to the other, Gaisberg was smoking a cigarette and Jelka was mumbling to herself, just having dropped a stitch. Elgar, I sensed, was suffering.

Then the competition arrived in the form of a jazz band on a passing *bâteau-mouche*. I wondered, desperately, how Elgar would react. He didn't move a muscle, just continued leaning against the gramophone, doing the only thing a true Brit would do – stick it out. Mercifully, by the time side three was spinning on the turntable the competition was almost out of sight.

The next four minutes were the longest I have ever known. They were never-ending; they were an eternity. And to make matters worse, a fresh breeze had sprung up. Finally the agony came to an end. I wondered if I should break the silence, but I simply could not think of a word to say. And neither it seemed could anyone else – except Delius.

'Thank you, Sir Edward,' he said solemnly. 'Your daughter must be an exceptionally wondrous child. I shall treasure these records for ever.'

I think we were all more or less stunned by his reaction and even more so by that of Elgar, who walked across to Delius and, without a word, took him gently by the shoulders and kissed him lightly on both cheeks. At this Gaisberg said, 'Bravo', and started to applaud. Jelka and I joined in, and soon everyone was smiling.

'Now it's my turn. It's time for one of my favourites,' said Delius like a eager child.

'What'll it be, Fred?' said Jelka, springing to her feet. 'I think the First Cuckoo is in here somewhere. Let me take a look.' And she started rummaging in the gramophone cabinet.

'No, not that, Jelka, not today,' he admonished. 'There should be a ten-inch record there somewhere. Play that. You know, "Old Man River" sung by the Radio Revellers.'

And much to everyone's surprise (and relief), Jelka found it straight away and in next to no time everyone was dancing – around Delius: Jelka and I, Gaisberg and the manservant, and Elgar and the maid. I could see he had his eye on her from the start.

And here I'm afraid my little story must end, for, sad to say, I disgraced myself once again and was sent back to England prematurely on the overnight ferry.

TWENTY

The Last Muse

SPOONER, OUR JOURNALIST acquaintance who popped up every decade or so to get the dirt on Elgar, had surfaced once more for the Three Choirs Festival of 1933, held that year in Hereford. For, in common with many other observers, he was of the opinion that it might well be Elgar's farewell performance – the old boy was now seventy-five and not in the best of health. And then there had been rumours . . .

But before setting off from London Spooner had gone through the cuttings in the morgue at the *Chronicle*, where his mundane manner of reporting had earmarked him for early retirement. His object was to postpone that day by landing himself a scoop, and to that end he began to familiarize himself with Elgar's life since the false alarm in the war, when he had been accused of spying by Joe Kitcher, the odd-job man at Brinkwells. What a fiasco!

It was soon clear to Spooner that, musically, Elgar was undoubtedly an early wartime casualty. Three brief patriotic laments by the Belgian poet Cammaerts for recitation with orchestra were extremely weak and didn't survive the armistice. A ballet called *The Sanguine Fan* performed for charity during the same period was also soon forgotten, as was a short orchestral fantasy on Polish airs. Four seafaring poems by Rudyard Kipling that Elgar set to music were so pathetic that the poet had them banned.

Only one work was the equal of his pre-war output, and that was the Cello Concerto, premièred in 1919. Then, with the death of Lady Alice in the following year, his talent had dried up altogether until the fifth Pomp and Circumstance March, the 'Nursery Suite' and the announcement of a new symphony in 1932. The muse was courting again, it seemed, and to Spooner that meant one thing and one thing only – crumpet – and an order from the editor to *cherchez la femme*.

And that was why Spooner had sat through an Elgar double bill and was now sipping tea and circulating among the fans in the Cathedral Close, mobbing the great man for his autograph.

The fêted composer was in great good humour – beaming and affable – fresh from a triumphant performance of Gerontius. For though he was somewhat deficient in musical appreciation Spooner deduced that any conductor recalled to the podium a dozen times to tumultuous applause must have at least something going for him. And the fact that the entire orchestra rose to their feet to join in the general acclaim must count for something; for, in his experience, musicians were as cynical a bunch as the newspaper fraternity.

Yes, even Spooner was aware of the sense of occasion. The audience still swarming out of the dark cathedral into the late afternoon of an Indian summer buzzed around him like excited bees – determined to prolong the festive gathering as long as possible – aided and abetted by urns of tea and plates of sandwiches. This was an event of which Hereford was justly proud, and the picnic that invariably accompanied the last concert of a week of intense music-making was always a cause for rejoicing.

And as Spooner fortified his China tea with a discreet dash from a hip flask, his eye was caught by an attractive woman in a pretty frock seated on the grass scribbling away in an exercise book. Unlike most of the women present, she was bareheaded; but even so Spooner would not have spared her a second glance had he not seen her catch Elgar's eye and blow him a kiss which, surprise, surprise, he happily returned before beckoning her over. Dutifully she abandoned her pencil and paper, jumped to her feet and ran across to where the beleaguered old man was in danger of being engulfed.

Spooner made a snap decision. Striding through the surging crowd he snatched up the book and pencil and turned towards the writer as if to return them to her – but on seeing that nobody was paying him attention he veered off in a different direction and stuffed the stolen goods into a capacious pocket.

Then, from a safe distance, he turned his attention back to the odd couple – to see the woman discreetly extricating Elgar from the mob and leading him back to the spot she had only recently vacated. There she retrieved the light coat on which she had been sitting and started looking around for the missing articles. Spooner did not hang about to parade his guilt but set off as nonchalantly as possible to distance himself from his victim who was already showing some signs of distress. Spooner strode towards the city centre, the little exercise book almost burning a hole in his pocket. He entered the Rose and Crown inn and went straight to reception.

No, Sir Edward was not among the guests this year; try the Hereford Arms, he was told. He did so.

Yes, Sir Edward was in residence and has been for the entire week, volunteered the receptionist. He was due to depart the following day.

Yes, the gentleman was fortunate, for, as this was the last day of the festival, a few rooms had just become vacant. Room 58 could be thoroughly recommended. It was very quiet with a pleasant view of the park at 12s 6d a night including breakfast.

'Just for the one night, sir. Very well, I'll have the porter take care of your luggage. Oh, it will be coming on later. Very well, sir. If you will just sign the register I'll have you shown straight to your room.' And the clerk at the desk swung around the large register, dipped a pen in an inkwell and handed it to the shifty-looking guest who, while slowly filling in his own particulars at the foot of the right-hand page, committed a couple at the top of the left-hand page to his photographic memory.

Room 28 Sir Edward Elgar Bart, Marl Bank, Rainbow Hill, Worc.
Room 29 Mrs Vera Hockman, Robin Hill, Pine Coombe, Shirley, Croyden

Minutes later Spooner was sitting bolt upright on his wrought-iron bed savouring the moment of discovery that could well be the revelation of a lifetime and the prolongation of his tenure on the paper. Trembling, he opened the exercise book with the bright blue cover and flicked through its well-filled handwritten pages.

Putting on his spectacles, he started to read 'The Story of 7 November 1931'.

And what of the hapless author, still scouring the Cathedral Close, now all but deserted? Her immediate panic had long since given way to despondency and resignation. And there were tears in her eyes as she took in the lonely figure of Elgar, sitting patiently on a park bench, resting his chin on his gloved hands while clutching the top of his ivory-handled walking-stick. He looked so pathetic, poor man, his recent triumph draining away minute by minute, owing entirely to her mindless stupidity. With all the crowds of well-wishers gone, he seemed lonely and abandoned. Still, she would make it up to him tonight back at the hotel; that's if he were up to it, of course.

'No luck, I'm afraid, Eddie,' she said, approaching him forlornly.

'Never mind, love,' he replied, struggling to his feet. 'We can telephone the police station back at the hotel. It's quite likely someone handed it in.'

'I just hope it doesn't fall into the wrong hands,' she said with a sigh, taking his arm.

'I thought you were writing it with an eye to publication,' he replied, as they strolled away.

'I was – eventually.'

This was followed by a heavy silence, finally broken by Elgar. 'When I've kicked the bucket, I presume.'

'Oh, Eddie, don't be so morbid. They've already planned next year's programme in Worcester with the première of your new symphony.'

'Your symphony,' he said softly, squeezing her arm.

'Our symphony,' she replied, impulsively kissing his cheek.

'Careful, darling,' he said, quickly glancing around.

'Oh, Eddie, don't take on so; it was only a peck.'

But Elgar would not be mollified. The disappearance of the book continued to worry him. 'I trust that in your jottings you exercised the necessary discretion.'

'It's really just a record of how we met, et cetera et cetera.; there's nothing wrong in that, surely,' she reasoned. 'You met plenty of strangers at the same time, if you recall – not only a humble violinist but every member of the Croydon Philharmonic Orchestra.'

'But I do not recall making love to them,' added Elgar with a smile. 'Did you include that in your et cetera et cetera?'

'Don't worry. My innocent little book could be read aloud at your average Sunday School class.'

'Oh dear,' laughed Elgar, 'that's where I first learned the facts of life – and not from the Reverend Father, I hasten to add. Now let's step on the gas, please. I'm dying for a large scotch and soda.'

In his bedroom in the Royal Hereford Hotel a disgruntled Spooner tossed the little blue book to the foot of the bed. For, though this humble musician in the

Croydon Philharmonic had bared her soul, it was by no means certain that she had bared her body. Yes, the handwritten account of Elgar's infatuation with a married woman forty years his junior was as detailed as it was passionate, but on the one occasion where it was recorded that Elgar called her his 'lover' she had added 'and friend'.

For over a year they had had innumerable meetings – not only whenever Elgar came to London but also at his home in Worcester. Spooner wondered about witnesses and the possibility of interviewing them. Of their various mutual acquaintances Carice Elgar was certainly the key, her role being that of confidante and chauffeur – she was forever driving them all over the place. Then there were Vera's two young children and her estranged husband who was working abroad – not much chance there, he reasoned.

What to do? Camp outside their respective bedroom doors all night in the hope of hearing the tell-tale sound of creaking bedsprings? Or perhaps he could bribe a chambermaid for a report on the state of the bedclothes in the morning. It wouldn't be the first time he had tried that ploy.

Daft idea; truth to tell, he seriously doubted the old man's ability to get it up . . . and yet there was a rumour flying around the musical establishment that there was an illegitimate child lurking somewhere behind the scenes. That would also warrant investigation.

Then he considered the notion of confronting them, possibly in the bar or in the lounge or the restaurant – but on what pretext? Why, the obvious one, of course – that he'd come across the book and tracked her down. She'd be overjoyed, jokingly offer to reward him and ask him his price . . . to which he would respond in all seriousness, 'An exclusive interview, Miss Hockman'; surely an offer she could not refuse if she really wanted her book back. After that – well, he had a way of getting women to open up, didn't he?

So, determined on a course of action, he looked in the mirror, tightened his tie, ran his fingers through his hair, tucked the little blue book under the mattress, left the room and went downstairs.

First, he looked in the bar – no sign of them. Then he wandered into the lounge – plenty of couples consulting menus but not the one that mattered. Perhaps they were already at dinner, prior to an early night. No, they weren't there either.

'Can I help you, sir?' asked the head waiter.

'I was hoping to join Sir Edward for dinner,' said Spooner nonchalantly.

'Yes, he was due in at eight o'clock, sir, but I've just had a message from reception to cancel the booking.'

'Cancel the booking? Whatever for?'

'I'm afraid I've no idea, sir. May I show you to a table?'

But Spooner was already on his way to reception.

'I was expecting to join Sir Edward for dinner,' said Spooner abruptly to the man behind the desk, 'and have just been told there's been a cancellation.'

'That's correct, sir,' replied the receptionist quietly. 'Sir Edward is no longer with us.'

'What?' exclaimed Spooner, assuming the worst.

'What I mean, sir,' said the receptionist, observing his alarm, 'is that Sir Edward has taken his leave.'

'What do you mean? Stop speaking in riddles. I'm a great personal friend of his and I demand to know what's happened.'

Fearful of a scene, the receptionist hastily replied, *sotto voce*, 'Please, sir, do keep your voice down. Sir Edward has recently suffered a stroke. Not more than a half-hour ago I saw him going into the bar with a young lady, chipper as you like; next thing I know there's an ambulance at the door.'

'Where did they go?'

'I'm afraid I've no idea, sir,' said the receptionist with a straight face.

Fucking liar, thought Spooner as he made for the telephone.

TWENTY-ONE

A Daughter's Revenge

SPOONER NEVER TRACKED them down. They certainly weren't in Hereford – he tried every hospital and nursing home in the vicinity. In fact, they were at Marl Bank, Elgar's home in Worcester some twenty-five miles to the north-east.

The stroke wasn't serious, but Elgar's back was giving him hell. Exploratory surgery revealed a malignant tumour and a life expectancy of weeks rather than months.

Vera spun feverishly into a kind of denial. She spent as much time with him as possible, but work commitments curtailed her visits drastically; and of course Elgar was unable to leave the house or even his bed of late. There was, however, a regular exchange of letters, including one from an excited Vera with the news that an anonymous benefactor had returned her blue exercise book. No note of explanation was included – nothing.

So Spooner's little secret died with him, and his editor, who – while commending the journalist on his enterprise – elected to leave well enough alone. For one thing, there was no concrete proof of hanky-panky and, additionally, it was rumoured that the old boy was not long for this world. Mud-slinging might be in danger of boomeranging. Still, if nothing else, it did win Spooner a reprieve from early retirement – if only by six months, by which time Elgar was history.

And history is what the old man was conscious of, as he dragged out his last remaining days – gazing out of the window at the end of his bed, with misty eyes.

The garden was beneath his field of vision but not so Worcester Cathedral, scene of many triumphs, or the Malvern Hills five miles in the distance, source of his inspiration. In his mind he climbed those beloved hills daily, sometimes alone, sliding down the grassy slopes on a tea tray; occasionally with Carice, flying a kite; but, more often than not, hand in hand with his beloved wife, Alice – now a wistful memory.

Rudyard Kipling's 'The Widower', with its promise of the reunion of husband and wife after death, was a prayer that assuaged – somewhat – his guilt and gave him comfort. So did the memories of his 'friends pictured within' his music (the very phrase he had used in dedicating the 'Enigma') whenever Carice played recordings of his works on the gramophone.

A state-of-the-art cabinet model, the gramophone had been thoughtfully provided by HMV, who had done the nation a great service over the years by commissioning the composer to conduct and record most of his extensive repertory, from Salut d'Amour to the Dream of Gerontius. Elgar even supervised a studio recording far away in London from his sickbed by telephone, but hopes for the completion of the Third Symphony (Vera's symphony), which had been commissioned by the BBC, were not to be realized. The suspicion that plans were afoot for the work to be completed by other hands after his death gave Elgar growing cause for alarm. He made Carice solemnly promise never to let this happen, and as long as there was a breath left in her body she was true to her word.

And as the days dragged by and the pain increased, the things that gave him solace were music and morphine and the dreams they induced.

A particular favourite was his symphonic study 'Falstaff', one of his last great works, completed just before the war. Those who knew Elgar well saw in it not so much an evocation of Shakespeare's flawed hero but something closer to a self-portrait of the composer himself. And there were indisputable similarities: the bluff good humour, a love of the Gloucestershire countryside, an eye for the ladies, a taste for a refreshing tankard of cider and – on a more serious note – even rejection by the establishment.

But what constantly surprised Elgar about his 'Falstaff' was that, with only one exception, nobody seemed to have recognized the Sunbeam Bicycle theme that cropped up from time to time as a compelling leitmotif. Surely that memorable tune could be nothing else but the exhilaration you felt on speeding along, up hill and down dale, with a fresh breeze in your face and a pretty girl at your side – the pretty girl being Rosa Burley . . . the only one, by the way, ever to note the obvious.

Reliving these joyous rides invariably induced nostalgia for a lost love, one of many. Maybe he should have married Rosa after all. But then he would never have taken up with Vera – or would he? Marriage to Alice had never stood in the way of his heart's desire before, but Rosa was made of sterner stuff and would have put her foot down, no question.

Sometimes it seemed to him that he had lived a lifetime with each of his loves alone, instead of all at once. That would have been a lot of lifetimes. No wonder he was tired.

But it was the Violin Concerto that gave him the greatest pleasure, despite the flaw on side four of the record enshrining the climax of the slow movement – Carice had accidentally scratched it while impatiently removing the pick-up one day. She hastily ordered a replacement, but it didn't survive the Royal Mail and arrived in pieces. So Elgar had to put up with a constant click-click-click – an impediment he grouchily learned to live with.

Carice, keeping her own counsel, looked upon it as poetic justice. The piece reminded her of her father's unalloyed pleasures at the expense of her mother's stoic pain – horribly undeserved, brought about by that unholy liaison with Windflower. She earnestly hoped that each click would be like a disturbing prick of conscience to the old man. And to a certain extent it was – he had never fully outgrown the guilt over his treatment of Alice, even if he had eventually come to live with it.

Other works that afforded him pleasure were the two little Dream Children idylls composed in 1902. Here is the passage Elgar quoted at the head of the score:

And while I stood gazing, both the children gradually grew fainter and fainter to my view, receding and still receding, till nothing at last but two mournful features were seen in the uttermost distance, which, without speech, strangely impressed upon me the effects of speech: "We are not of Alice, nor of thee, nor are we children at all. We are nothing, less than nothing, and dreams. We are only what might have been."

'What might have been' had he married Alice Stuart-Wortley, perhaps. These child phantoms certainly resembled her, and when Carice played the recording of the piece, directly after the Violin Concerto, it was like having his secret family about the house, a situation Carice grew fully aware of, even as her disapproval grew with it. Oh, how she longed for someone to shake her up

– like a bottle of fizz – she'd go off with a pop that would blow the top off her father's phony image for ever.

Her husband would never do as catalyst; he rarely touched her and was more concerned with matters agricultural than musical and rarely left his farm in the Midlands. She had met him shortly after her mother died, on the only holiday she'd ever been allowed to take on her own. They got to know each other in Switzerland – the one couple in the hotel who couldn't ski, which turned out to be the only thing they had in common. But after a lifetime of repression Carice was desperate, and swapped a life as an unpaid nurse caring for a hypochondriac parent to be an unpaid nurse to a sickly husband.

Nothing changes. True, there was a paid nurse to tend to Elgar's needs in the day, when he seemed to sleep most of the time. But it was at night, when he was often at his most demanding, that Carice was on duty.

There he was, yelling and ringing that wretched hand-bell again. What now? She dragged herself out of bed, pulled on her slippers, climbed into her dressing-gown, lit a candle (he hated the electric light) and made her way along the corridor to his room. The window was wide open; it was like an ice house. That nurse! She closed it immediately without comment.

'I want to hear side nine of the Symphony in A flat,' he commanded huskily.

Carice set down the candle and sorted through the records.

'And for God's sake, be more careful this time. We don't want any more concertos for clicks and orchestra,' he croaked.

'Do you want a drink?' Carice ventured. 'You sound a little hoarse.'

Elgar neighed like one, gave a little chuckle and said, 'Been shouting for you for half an hour. Going deaf in your old age, are you?'

Carice remained silent and put on the record with haste, with the result that the slow movement of the First Symphony sounded slower than ever.

'Come on, muggins,' growled Elgar. 'It's not a fucking funeral march. Wind the bugger up, for Christ's sake.'

With an unvoiced sigh Carice obediently wound the handle until the spring of the motor was tight and the music flowed serenely – but not serenely enough for the tetchy old man.

'The speed control needs adjusting. It's too fast. Surely you know how it goes after all these years . . . How many is it?'

The question may have been rhetorical, but as Carice made the requisite adjustment she answered all the same. 'Twenty-five years, Father. A quarter of a century.'

'That's it, rub it in,' he snapped before lapsing into silence.

The music was soporific. Carice nearly dozed off. Only the needle swishing in the run-off groove saved her. Hastily she removed the pick-up.

'Did I ever tell you what inspired that passage?' asked Elgar.

Carice wanted to scream – oh, if only she had the nerve! But 'Yes, Papa,' she said evenly. 'It was something you heard down by the river.'

'Ah, but do you know exactly where, my girl,' he said in a superior sort of voice.

Of course she knew where. Hadn't he told her a thousand times? Hadn't she actually been there with him at the time? Cooling his bottle of beer in the shallows, still as a statue, her bum going numb on the stones lest – in trying for a modicum of comfort – she disturb a pebble and bring down his wrath.

But still she felt compelled to give him the pleasure of revealing his secret all anew, and remained silent.

'I'll tell you then,' he whispered. 'But it must be our secret. Promise not to tell.'

'Promise, Father,' she replied softly.

'Well, it's where the Severn meets the Teme,' said Elgar, as if revealing the secret of creation. 'And that's where I want to be buried. That is my dying wish, the wish of a free spirit.'

'Oh, Papa, please, please don't talk like that. You'll get better, I know you will,' protested Carice in agony. 'Shall I put on the next side?'

'Don't change the subject,' said Elgar. 'You will abide by my wishes, d'you hear me? Now get off to bed. You're keeping me up with your chatter.'

Carice did not reply but forced herself to kiss her father's cheek before leaving the room.

The next day Elgar had a relapse, and despite the fact that he had angrily rejected God and all his works Carice sent for a priest to perform the last rites. If he had been conscious at the time Elgar might well have rejected them. But as it was, Carice supervised his burial three days later at the Catholic church in Little Malvern – beside his long-suffering wife Lady Caroline Alice.

There were few mourners. No music was played. None of the muses turned up. Carice cried – with relief.

TWENTY-TWO

The Last Laugh

*A*ND AS HE slowly regained consciousness, Elgar gradually became aware of his surroundings. He was lying in a pool of mud, on what appeared to be a battlefield. There was music, familiar music. Music from Wagner's *Götterdämmerung – The Twilight of the Gods*. Was it Siegfried's Funeral March? Yes! Trumpets and drums sounded a noble lament in memory of the fallen hero.

Now the music was changing in mood and tempo, becoming ever more upbeat, purposeful, pulsating. Hoofbeats blending with the music were joined by the cries of Amazonian women whom Elgar recognized as the Valkyries – female goddesses dedicated to snatching dead heroes from the war-torn earth and carrying them off to the glory of Valhalla.

The ride on that old warhorse of orchestral virtuosity was one of the most uncomfortable journeys Elgar had ever experienced and one of the most ignominious. Slung across the saddle with a view of galloping hooves and bloodstained soil, accompanied by the stentorian bellow of a sixteen-stone soprano, had not been his idea of life in the hereafter.

Suddenly the nightmarish motion stopped and the reluctant passenger was pitched unceremoniously to the ground. The sudden jolt winded him, causing him to screw up his eyes in pain. When he opened them it was to see a familiar face bending over him.

'Good God, Jaeger,' exclaimed Elgar. 'What the hell are you doing here? You're supposed to be dead.'

'I'm the reception committee. The intention is to welcome newcomers in a manner fitting to their station and in a way that won't freak them out.'

'Freak them out,' repeated Elgar. 'What on earth do you mean?'

'In modern parlance, "to freak someone out" means to really upset them, and please do remember that we are not "on earth" any more. And another word of advice – I wouldn't mention the word "hell" more than you have to, for reasons that I hope will never become obvious.'

'Thank you for the tip,' said Elgar. 'Now, tell me more; tell me why I've ended up in what appears to be a randy German's idea of the hereafter? No offence, old sport.'

'None taken,' said Jaeger. 'I should have thought it was obvious. Just think.'

Elgar did so and, much to his surprise, came up with a quick answer that felt like clarity itself.

'Could it be because I really owe everything to the Fatherland, and my music follows in the great German tradition?' ventured Elgar.

'Of course,' said Jaeger with a smile. 'Now tell me, what can I do for you?'

'Draw me a bath,' said Elgar.

Herr Jaeger nearly corpsed himself. 'Whatever for?' he exclaimed. 'Do you really feel in need of one, or is it just force of habit? Be honest, now.'

'Look at me,' said Elgar. 'I'm covered in mud.'

'Another thing you have to learn,' explained Jaeger, 'is to stop making stock assumptions. Taste it!'

'What?' said Elgar in disbelief.

'Come along, lick your fingers.'

For a moment Elgar looked at Jaeger as if he doubted his sanity, after which he decided to humour him and take a tentative lick. Hmm. It was the most delicious chocolate he had ever tasted.

'See,' said Jaeger. 'Now, I'll ask you again – just close your eyes and tell me how you feel.'

Elgar did as he was bid and . . . began to feel a warm glow and a sense of well-being that had him beaming in satisfaction. 'It's rather fun being dead,' he remarked. 'I haven't felt as happy as this since those summer days I spent on the banks of the Teme, dreaming the day away with dear little Carice.'

And when he finally opened his eyes, there it was, the event exactly as he had described it, with the addition of two extra figures – himself and Jaeger. 'I say, won't she see us?' said Elgar in alarm. 'I'd hate to frighten her.'

'Don't worry,' said Jaeger comfortingly. 'Carice doesn't believe in ghosts; and anyway this is just a memory.'

'And one of my most cherished,' said Elgar. 'Though I must confess Carice doesn't look too happy.'

'Because she knows full well that there is no room for her in your precious daydreams. Like her mother, she felt excluded, knowing you had other women on your mind.'

'I'm all too aware of my faults, thank you, my friend,' said Elgar a bit testily, 'and given another chance would make full amends, I promise you.'

'But the life that late you led was another chance. Your second, in fact,' said Jaeger, 'as everyone who has read any of those excellent biographies on you must well know – providing they've embraced a little Buddhism or Hinduism or reincarnationism on the side, of course.'

For a moment Elgar was nonplussed, even disbelieving; until he remembered the numerous occasions in which he had experienced a weird feeling of *déjà vu* – of numerous events with which he was vaguely familiar. A weird feeling of significance would overcome him, but what it meant, he'd never had a clue.

'If what you say is true, old man, all I can say is I made a bigger hash of it the second time around than I did originally,' said Elgar. 'But surely, I wouldn't go on making these same mistakes indefinitely, would I?'

'Mistakes are of little importance, Eddie,' Jaeger told him. 'We're talking about transgression here. Are you aware of how many sins you confessed to during your life?'

'Who's counting?' mumbled Elgar, feebly.

'And do you know who those sins were committed against?'

'No need to rub it in,' said Elgar aloud, knowing full well to whom Jaeger was referring. 'But I can promise you that, given another chance, I swear to God that I would make full amends; ditch all those stupid dream girls and give both Alice and Carice the love and respect they deserve. As God is my witness.'

'Well, it saddens me to have to say this, Eddie, it really does, but though I was not here at the time I have it on good authority that those were the exact words you used the last time around. What do you say to that?' Jaeger waited patiently as Elgar seemed to take almost an age to reply.

'God is not mocked,' he said finally.

'Good answer,' said Jaeger, with a smile of relief. 'It has saved you from an eternity of purgatory. You will be returning to life on earth again, I can assure you.'

'Thank God,' said Elgar, dropping to his knees.

'In fact, you will be returning not once but twice.'

At this Elgar lifted his eyes to heaven in gratitude.

But Jaeger had not finished. 'First, in the body of your daughter Carice. And, secondly, in the body of your wife Caroline Alice.'

Elgar winced, knowing full well that he had just been condemned to not one season in hell but two. He suffered them instantly and, before he knew it, was about to enter the presence of God.

'She was only kidding,' whispered Jaeger.

Delius:

A Moment with Venus

Contents

DELIUS: A MOMENT WITH VENUS

ONE — Eventyr (Once Upon a Time) *135*

TWO — North-Country Sketches *139*

I — The Wind Soughs in the Trees

II — Winter Landscape

III — Dance

IV — The March of Spring

THREE — Florida Suite *143*

I — Daybreak

II — Dance

III — By the River

IV — Sunset – Near the Plantation

V — At Night

FOUR — Paris: The Song of a Great City *149*

FIVE — Life's Dance *153*

SIX — Brigg Fair *157*

SEVEN — Over the Hills and Far Away *161*

EIGHT — On Hearing the First Cuckoo of Spring *165*

NINE — Song of Summer *169*

TEN — Song on the High Hills *173*

ELEVEN — Summer Night on the River *177*

TWELVE — Requiem *179*

THIRTEEN — The Walk to the Paradise Gardens *183*

FOURTEEN — Double Concerto *185*

FIFTEEN — In a Summer Garden *188*

ONE

Eventyr
(Once Upon a Time)

O NCE UPON A time there was a rotund man with a monocle and a heavy German accent who was father to a family of fourteen offspring, a couple of whom never survived childhood. They were the unlucky ones in so far that they were never to hear even one of Papa's bizarre bedtime stories.

The memory of them came to mind – fleetingly – as, with his wife Jelka, Delius attended a performance of Ibsen's *Peer Gynt* in Trondheim towards the end of the Great War. Norway had long won a place in his heart ever since the days of his youth when he had travelled there on business for Papa. And was not his good friend Grieg the country's most illustrious musical ambassador? And the brilliant incidental music he had especially composed and was now conducting would have been well worth the journey alone even if the refugee couple hadn't decided to settle there for the duration of the present European conflict.

That momentous evening proved to be a kick-start that had sparked Delius's creative talents (which recent events had rendered idle) back into life again. Every number, from the evocative strains of Morning to the sly sensuality of Anitra's Dance, had delighted him, but In the Hall of the Mountain King with its demonic chorus of cavorting trolls had been an absolute knockout. These creatures of myth and legend had intrigued Delius ever since Jelka had given him a volume of Asbjørnsen's and Moe's folk tales as a Christmas present last year. And now his good friends Grieg and Ibsen had joined Jelka in pointing the way for his next opus.

Though his music is generally considered evocative, Delius had thus far avoided a purely narrative programme in his works. But having already decided to call it Eventyr – Norwegian for 'once upon a time' – he had no option but to tell some sort of tale leading up to a musical finale that spelled out 'happy ever after'. Where to begin? The possibilities were endless. The contenders could be counted in their hundreds, 'Babes in the Wood', 'Beauty and the Beast', 'Jack and the Beanstalk', 'Thumbelina', 'The Little Match Girl', 'Big Claus and Little Claus', 'The Cow Girl and the Troll' (Jelka's suggestion), 'Goldilocks and the Three Bears' ... He rejected them all and had almost opted for 'Hansel and Gretel' when he was reminded (Jelka again) that Humperdinck had already written a very popular opera on the subject. She also poured cold water upon his second choice, 'Cinderella' – Rossini had already produced the fabled glass slipper years ago. At this juncture Fred had become very angry and seriously considered abandoning the idea, until a letter from his sister triggered memories of childhood and, inevitably, Papa's bedtime stories – totally unknown outside the family circle they were a mine of inspiration. And he would pay tribute to the old storyteller by dedicating his symphonic poem to the one who had stood by him through thick and thin despite his serious objections to Fred's chosen career. He owed the old man more than he could ever repay. Eventyr would be an acknowledgement of that debt. But it would be his secret. He would tell no one – not even Jelka. So, closing his eyes, he wished himself back to the big front room of his childhood home in Bradford with all his siblings grouped around Father sitting in a big armchair sipping port in front of a roaring fire, about to launch into a new and exciting tale that, according to custom, was based on fact. Father placed a finger to his lips for complete silence and began.

'Once upon a time when your dear mutter and me came to Gross Britannia on our honeymoon ve visited an area called ze Lake District. Ve heard it vas a second Bavaria and so it proved to be der case. Ve felt quite at home zere, not only was ze scenery similar but so vere der myths and der legends of der area. Now you all heard of der Rhinemaidens who guarded der Rhinegold. Vell der is a river zere called der Derwent ver der vere drei sisters named Millicent, Maude und Mavis who vere der guardians of some very special geltfish vot lived under der bridge at der picturesque klein village of Grange in der valley auf Borrowdale – der most magical platz in all der land.

'Vell ein fine spring morgen dere vas a May Tag Vestival down der valley at Castle Crag to vich all der sisters wanted to go. But vun had to stay behind to guard der geltfish. So zey all drew lots with der result zat it was poor Mavis who drew der short straw. Never mind, she vould go another time. So off ze two lucky sisters vent, following der river through der dappled voods as dey picked dair vay through moss-covered boulders zat littered der valley.

'On zair vay zey ver passed by ein gnomeska mench on a raft who raised his hat in greeting. Zis vas Elf Scratcher who lived in a cave further up der valley. Ze girls giggled and vent zair merry vay through woods of dappled sunlight.

'Meanwhile, as Elf Scratcher drifted down der Derwent on his vay to Grange to do his shopping, a plan was forming in his evil mind – for a good gnome he most certainly vas not.

'By now time Millicent und Maude had reached der foot of Castle Crag – ein grosser tower of granite zat soared some drei hundred and seventy metres in der sky.'

'What's that in feet and inches,' the children chorused.

'Vot difference does it make?' retorted Papa, anxious to continue his tale.

'They don't teach us metric units at school, Papa,' Herman replied.

'Multiply three und ein bit,' Papa snapped, 'und zer du haff der answer.' And while the children attempted some tricky mental arithmetic father Julius continued.

'From ze top of der summit came der sound of music und merrymaking vich grew louder with each new step der sisters took as they huffed and puffed zair way up der twisting und turning track zat eventually led to der top. And who should zey see zair tanzing mit der locals but Robin Hood und his Merry mench – und you all know who zey vere, don't you?'

A chorus of 'Ya, ya' came in quick response with the *kinder* all calling out their favourites:

'Friar Tuck.'

'Mädchen Marion.'

'Will Scarlet.'

'Klein John and Big Jim.'

'Big Yim I never heard of,' said Papa to baby Adolf, 'but if you vant him you shall haff him.'

'Tell us more about Elf Scratcher,' piped up young Karen.

'Ah, I'm glad you asked,' said Papa. 'For by now Elf had reached Grange and had tied his raft to a tree close to der bridge where Mavis was singing sweetly.

'"That's a pretty song," said Elf. "Is it meant for me?"

'"It's a love song," Mavis said, smiling sweetly.

'"Zen you may kiss me," said Elf Scratcher, boldly taking her hand, closing his eyes and puckering up his lips.

'"Nein, nein, nein," shouted Mavis pushing him into the river mit ein splash.

'"Help, help! I can't swim!" he lied.

'"Oh, do stop splashing about!" Mavis exclaimed. "You're frightening der fish."

'"Save me, save me! I'm drowning!" he cried, starting to flounder.'

'I thought you said they were goldfish,' laughed Fritz. 'So how did they turn into flounders?'

'Zat's just ein colloquialism,' replied Father. 'Don't interrupt!'

'And did he drown?' asked Clare.

'No, of course not,' said Father testily. 'He vas just pretending. All der time he was *floundering* about he vas secretly filling his pockets mit der geltfish.'

'Why couldn't they just swim out again?' queried Joseph.

'Because he had buttons on der pockets, dat's vy!'

'Papa, I do believe you're making it all up,' interjected Paula.

'Vot you mean, making it up? Would I really bozzer to make up ein fairy story? Are you calling your own fazer ein fibber?'

'Father's a fibber,' Max piped up as one by one all the others joined in. 'Father's a fibber, Father's a fibber.' Their chant nearly raised the rafters until Father was finally driven from the room screaming. 'No strudel tonight! You go straight to bed mit no strudel, mit no strudel!'

'Mit no strudel. Mit no strudel,' they chanted amid peals of laughter as they all stamped their way upstairs to bed.

And it was a least a week before a disgruntled Papa could be cajoled into finishing the story – which of course ended happily ever after. But not before Elf Scratcher had scraped all the gold off the scales of the goldfish and incarcerated Mavis in the local church tower, where she had sounded the alarm on the church bells calling her sisters and Robin and his Merry Men to the rescue. It's all there in the music if you listen very, very carefully.

TWO

North-Country Sketches

I AUTUMN: THE WIND SOUGHS IN THE TREES

Shifting woodwinds, barely audible, suggesting mist rising over moors shrouded in mystery. Pianissimo strings creep in like a ghost.

Clare Delius, the composer's favourite sister, seated at his side, gently took his hand in her own. It was a special occasion, Sir Thomas Beecham was conducting the first performance of a score that held special significance for them. It was in effect a 'love song', and it was their secret.

From childhood they had escaped from the strictures of the family home and the smoke of Bradford on to the Yorkshire moors whenever possible, a habit that had continued until Fritz left home in his early twenties and continued sporadically thereafter.

One of Clare's greatest treasures was the first love song he had ever written for her to perform when he was still a schoolboy long ago.

Now the wind was surely soughing in the trees − a particularly evocative moment recalling flights through the air with Fred in a magic wood near the little village of Ilkley. It was here that Fred had constructed a magnificent swing just big enough for the two of them. And now the music was bearing them aloft again through a shifting curtain of multicoloured autumn leaves.

She gripped her brother's hand even tighter as she continued to reach the heights in a 'heart in the mouth' state of suspended animation. She went up, up, up and never wanted to come down again.

II WINTER LANDSCAPE

'I do,' said Fritz. 'I love you.'

Fritz and Clare were out walking on the moors. It was snowing and Clare was melancholy.

'You've been neglecting me of late,' she chided.

'I've been busy in the office.'

'Busy flirting,' she countered with a wan smile.

'Business relations. Just obeying Father's orders. You know his motto: "Keep the workers happy".'

This was not the answer Clare was hoping for. Fritz had put his foot in it, and for several minutes they walked on in silence – caressed by the lightly falling snow. To Fritz, fully alive and all aglow, each flake was like a burning kiss; to Clare they were wet and impersonal, like the kisses of a maiden aunt. In her early twenties and still unmarried she was beginning to feel like one.

'Nobody loves me,' she repeated in tones laden with regret.

It touched Fritz profoundly and caused him to take in the scene before him with different eyes. The sensual rise and fall of the hills clothed in swansdown heralding the advent of spring was transformed into a shroud, cloaking the death of summer's promise.

'Nobody loves me,' Clare repeated in the same tone, accompanied spontaneously in her brother's mind by a series of notes resulting in a theme both lyrical and soulful. Inspired, Fritz gave voice to this most haunting of melodies in words as uplifting as they were reassuring.

'I truly love thee,' he sang much to Clare's surprise and delight. She smiled, she glowed and melted as Fritz daringly kissed her on the lips.

It was one of the most magical moments of her life that she was reliving now as the orchestra repeated that phrase over and over while the snow continued to fall in the concert hall as Thomas Beecham and the orchestra caressed that memory with the utmost finesse. Neither brother nor sister dared face each other. That was long ago and Clare was now a married woman.

III DANCE

A complete change of tempo lightened Clare's mood. To start with, no specific pictures came to mind; she was simply content to enjoy being in close proximity to her beloved brother (whom she saw too infrequently) until suddenly she was airborne again – not in their secret wood but close by at an annual summer fair at Ilkley they attended regularly when living at home together. She and Fritz were sharing one of the big swing-boats, which their efforts on the crossed ropes were sending higher than any of their neighbours – far higher. And – aaah . . . that never-to-be-forgotten sensation when at the apex of their flight they were suspended in time between heaven and earth but a little bit closer to heaven, surely . . . aaah . . . Yes, definitely, Fritz had captured it for ever in his music. She felt that prolonged sensation of ecstasy deep in her tummy once again after all those years. And then moving in a completely different orbit as they spun in a heady dance to the swirl of the village band. She wished it would never end . . . But surely that was twilight in the music and the twinkle of fairy lights.

And before they knew it they had missed the last conveyance back home to Bradford. They would have to put up in the local inn. It was packed. They had to share a bed. She remembered Fritz leaning across her to blow out the candle. The music faded away in a curl of smoke.

IV THE MARCH OF SPRING

Oh dear, here was the last movement. Too soon it would all be over. What to expect? Hadn't Mahler opened his third symphony with a Spring March – all trombone and German band? All bombast and birdsong.

Well, the birdsong was there right enough in Fred's version – wasn't the oboe giving voice to the call of a thrush?

And all at once there she was on the moors again listening to Fred going 'shush' with his fingers to his lips. Right away she froze like a statue, but Spot the dog went on barking till Fred picked him up in his arms, which shocked the frisky animal into silence, leaving the thrush to rhapsodize unhindered in the crisp spring air. She would never forget the joy on her brother's face as he mentally made a note of it.

Yes, she remembered the occasion well. By then, she was married with a small family living just outside Skipton in a rambling mansion that Charlotte Brontë had taken as a model for Gateshead Hall in Jane Eyre.

It was very spooky, she thought to herself, and I am not surprised that Fred was always on the look-out for the ghost of Mrs Rochester on every stormy night. This experience caused Fred to develop an interest not only in Charlotte but the rest of the Brontë brood, which in turn led to a growing desire to visit the place of their birth in the vicarage at the nearby village of Haworth. And, of course, he insisted that I accompany him for, though he never mentioned it, I firmly believe that he had come to regard us as soulmates just like Heathcliffe and Cathy in *Wuthering Heights*. True, we were both passionate about the moors, and hardly a day passed that we did not brave the elements on our travels of exploration. And the more the wind blew the more we loved it. Exhausting, yes, but it was always an excuse for a rest in the shelter of a jutting shelf of granite where Fred would comfort me in his arms. Now we are cuddled up in front of a roaring fire in the Black Bull where Branwell Brontë, the Vicar of Haworth's only son, a literary failure, used to drown his sorrows. Fred and I drink a toast to his memory with steaming rum toddies.

'Last orders,' shouts the genial landlord.

Time for us to go upstairs, as my heart beats faster . . .

Silence, then thunderous applause, and the conductor is pointing out Fred and encouraging him to acknowledge his due and take a bow.

Smiling shyly, he does so. The applause doubles. He turns to the person sitting on his left. It is his wife Jelka. He appears to be lifting her hand to his lips and . . . and . . . I'm afraid things are getting a little misty, I can't see clearly. I close my eyes, tight shut.

THREE

Florida Suite

I DAYBREAK

H E WAS GOING back to Salano Grove. It was early, the deck was all but deserted. This time tomorrow it would be packed – everyone craning their necks to get a first glimpse of the Statue of Liberty.

He wondered what his precious orange grove would look like after ten years of neglect – well, not total neglect if Albert Anderson, the Negro foreman he'd left in charge, was still around. Albert had never written, couldn't write, wouldn't write. But if it had all reverted to the jungle he would cut his losses and sell up or maybe try growing tobacco. He had heard there was more money in tobacco, and the climate wasn't right for oranges, anyway. Either way, he wasn't much bothered; the real reason for his trip was girl trouble – a tug of war between his fiancé Jelka Rosen and his mistress Princess Marie Leonie de Cystria, with Fritz the reluctant rope.

Peace at last – with both his hot-headed paramours left to cool their heels in Paris.

The first movement of his Florida Suite came to mind – cool, peaceful – pastel shades suffused by misty curtains of Spanish moss glimpsed through the bedroom window of his little cabin on the St Johns River. In less than a week he would be back there discovering its delights all over again.

II DANCE

The thought of renewed delights brought Lindy to mind – Lindy and the little half-caste piccaninny, rumour had it, was the fruit of their labours. Sex under the mosquito nets that invariably enveloped them had always been a sweaty business. In fact it was her sweat that first excited him when the Negro workers on his plantation had thrown a party to welcome their new master on the night of his arrival. He'd never seen such abandoned merrymaking. And the wildest reveller of all was also the most alluring. And could she dance! And could she shake that ass! The memory of that alone was well worth the five hundred dollars he'd paid for his first-class ticket. Fritz had missed her. Of all the women he'd enjoyed in the intervening years there had been no one to touch her.

He mentally willed her to be there on the jetty to greet him when the paddle steamer would give those two loud hoots to announce his arrival. What a thrill it would be to take her in his arms again and happily declare, 'Honey, I'm home.'

III BY THE RIVER

He leaned over the taffrail and watched the twin screws churn up the grey Atlantic. It was an occupation that stimulated old memories – memories of a paddle wheel churning up the muddy waters of the St Johns River on that thirty-mile trip downstream to the little town of Jacksonville.

He'd only been in residence at Salano Grove a month, and already he was missing his piano. True, he'd brought his violin along, but he couldn't compose on that, and already there were several Negro tunes he'd picked up from the hands that were ripe for development – and for that a keyboard was essential. Apart from that he was getting tired of his cramped little bungalow, while cultivating oranges was proving as tiresome as cultivating custom for the family wool business back home in England. He paled momentarily at the prospect of his father's reaction to this rebel act of truancy, should the old man ever get wind of it. No way would that pillar of Bradford society, born of Prussian aristocracy, ever permit a child of his to take up a career in music. For one thing, there was no money in it, but, above all, it was not a profession that could in any way command respect. *Gott in Himmel!* The thought of a son of his ending up fiddling for pennies in a grubby Bradford gutter was enough to make him almost die of shame. Now a position in the wool trade was another matter. And he would be following in his father's illustrious footsteps. And, being a dutiful son, Fritz had tried, he really had. Sadly he'd failed.

Equally saddened, Pater nevertheless had offered financial help on a business venture of the boy's own choosing. But why he fell in with Fritz's bizarre suggestion that he cultivate oranges in the New World was a mystery. But he probably reasoned that any business venture under the sun was preferable to the stigma of anything even remotely associated with music. For his part, Fritz simply wanted to get as far away from his parent's monocled Prussian eye as he possibly could.

Once in Jacksonville the errant youth made a beeline for the one and only piano emporium in town and had fun tinkling the ivories on everything in the showroom from a cottage upright to a Bechstein grand. And though not exactly a virtuoso he was competent enough to entice a few passers-by to linger at the door to enjoy his impromptu recital. One member of the *ad hoc* audience who remained longer than the rest was the local organist, Thomas Ward, a charming young man of thirty. Mightily impressed he introduced himself to Fritz and lent a sympathetic ear to the foreigner's tale of woe. In fact, he was so impressed that he offered to accompany the talented stranger back to his plantation and teach him the rudiments of composition. To Fritz this was nothing short of miraculous, and in next to no time the two new friends were entertaining passengers and crew alike on a cottage upright steaming south to Salano Grove. That meeting was to change Fritz's life.

IV SUNSET – NEAR THE PLANTATION

Such tranquillity; sitting on the veranda, sipping a mint julep and listening to the Negroes improvising on an old slave song, Fritz wished his pattern of life at Salano Grove would never change. Every waking day was a deeply felt pleasure of sensual aromas as Lindy kissed him gently on the forehead and set down a cup of freshly brewed Cuban coffee on his bedside table. Next would be a leisurely bath followed by further exploration into the wonderful world of music with Thomas Ward as his inspired guide. Then time out for a gastronomic picnic of Cajun chicken and saffron rice, followed by a little alligator hunting, an evening of relaxation and a night of loving Lindy.

But, alas, after an unforgettable six months it was all going to end. It was time for Thomas to go back to Jacksonville. And coincidentally Lindy had disappeared one day to nurse a sick relative. Life without them would be unbearable. He felt like a prisoner condemned to spend the rest of his days in a penal colony. But what was to stop him making his escape? The answer was the ball and chain that was the heavy weight of responsibility he felt towards his father. He simply could not just get up and walk away.

And then another miracle turned up – in the shape of his elder brother, Ernst. Disillusioned with sheep farming in New Zealand (he, too, was a disappointment to his dad), Ernst was on the look-out for a less active occupation.

'Try cultivating oranges,' enthused Fritz, 'you need never leave your rocking-chair.'

Easily convinced, Ernst soon got rocking while Fritz got packing and caught the next boat north to Jacksonville – with a completely clear conscience.

Once there he made a living singing (one might say 'sinning') in a synagogue. Rumour has it that converts to the Jewish faith increased significantly as word spread extolling the talents of a new Yiddish crooner in the community. Apparently most of the converts were female. Girl trouble again seems to have been responsible for his eventually taking refuge in the town of Danville five hundred miles north – where he made a big hit on the fiddle at the prestigious ladies' college.

It was here that he reputedly gave a ravishing performance of Mendelssohn's Violin Concerto, which won hundreds of hearts. Hardly surprising that just about nine months later it was time to leave town again. After that he simply disappeared and was tracked down only by the efforts of a private eye hired by a distraught parent, who begged the prodigal son to come back home again.

Once back in Bradford Fritz showered his dad with a deluge of musical diplomas, references and recommendations. This resulted in a deal being struck acceptable to both parties. Julius would finance lessons in composition at the famed Leipzig Conservatorium if Fritz would return to America on receipt of his graduation diploma. (Fat chance.)

But, though what Fritz got up to during the latter days of his stay in the United States will never be known, one thing is certain: the coaching he'd received from Thomas Ward began to pay off – he actually started composing music, inspired by impressions of Florida. An orchestral suite he'd started writing in the New World was finished off in the Old. And for the first time Fritz was to hear a real live orchestra play the music he'd only ever heard in his head.

The performance, which took place in a Leipzig Bierkeller, was a revelation. Of course, it wasn't the ideal venue for a world première, but at least it was affordable – a barrel of beer for the band and a bottle of champagne for the conductor.

This was the standard fee for any student brave enough to launch his fledgling works into the wide, wild world. Would Fritz's Florida Suite flop or fly? Fearful of getting the bird he had limited the odds by only admitting an audience of two, himself and a new friend, Edvard Grieg. Fritz hardly took his eyes off the great man's face during the entire performance. For the most part his expression was enigmatic, but there was no doubting his delight in the two Negro dance tunes interpolated into the score, particularly the second, which came at the conclusion of the third movement, Near the Plantation. Grieg even broke into spontaneous applause at the end of that. All things considered it wasn't a bad run-through, but Fritz vowed that if ever there was a repeat performance he would make sure the band had their reward after the performance, not before.

The best thing about it was learning from his mistakes and absorbing all the constructive criticism he got from Grieg. In fact, Grieg was a godsend, and it was solely because of his recommendation over brandy and cigars that Julius was persuaded to delay his son's departure after graduation day to the orange grove in favour of extended studies in Paris. And it was there that Fritz put the finishing touches to the last movement of his Florida Suite – a moody nocturne.

V AT NIGHT

Come nightfall Fritz had moved to the sharp end of the ship and was lost in contemplating the phosphorescent play of the bow waves when his travelling companion, a Norwegian fiddler called Halfdan Jebe (known by Jelka, who loathed him, as Halfwit Jebe), appeared at his side and said, 'I've just bumped into a dapper young fellow in a Savile Row suit who wants to go to bed with you.'

'Is he pretty?' asked Fritz, who never appeared phased by Halfdan's startling behaviour.

'Who said anything about "he"?' countered Halfdan, with a wink.

At this Fritz perked up. 'Explain,' he said, becoming somewhat uneasy.

But Halfdan was having fun. 'Of those two gross females you left behind in France, who would you least like to welcome aboard?'

Once he got over his initial surprise Fritz had it in one; the answer was Jelka, for with her fuller figure in no way could she possibly appear dapper even in a suit from Savile Row. In any case such shenanigans would definitely go against her dignity. Jelka could be a bit of a frump at times. No, it had to be the Princess; she was always up for a lark and would most likely look quite fetching in male attire. Having set out on the trip with the intention of shaking her off Fritz was anticipating the thrill of shacking up with her again. Such devotion was entirely admirable and should be handsomely rewarded.

But Halfdan took Fritz's silence for consternation and said reassuringly, 'Just say the word, my friend, and I'll see she takes a swim.'

Fritz smiled, despite himself, but before he could formulate a reply the lady in question materialized out of the darkness before them. She looked ravishing.

'Your cabin or mine?' she said to Fritz giving him the eye.

FOUR

Paris: The Song of a Great City

Mysterious city –
City of Pleasures
Of gay music and dancing
Of painted and beautiful women –
Wondrous city
Unveiling but to those who,
Shunning day
Live thru the night
And return home
To the sound of awakening streets
And the rising dawn

*T*HEY WERE AN odd couple 'Le Grand Anglais' and 'Le Petit Français', sleeping soundly together in the second-best bedroom of the premier brothel in the rue des Moulins. The little Frenchman, who was none other than Henri de Toulouse-Lautrec, had sacrificed his usual 'salon de luxe' in honour of visiting Victorian royalty. For this he was rewarded by the madam of the establishment with a freebie in the form of one Valentin le Desosse (Valentin the Double-jointed) who lay snoring between the two men who had spent an active night sharing her favours. The second lucky man, almost double the size of the midget painter, was Fritz Delius, a virtually unknown English composer.

Stirring languorously on the edge of sleep, the musician blinked into consciousness and slowly took in the unfamiliar surroundings as dawn stole in through the slender gaps in the heavy tobacco-laden curtains. Idly, he allowed his gaze to wander across the static features of the sleeping courtesan to the bearded profile of his generous little host still sleeping soundly. God! That little man could really go some. Delius had heard rumours about that notorious third leg, and now he pretty well had proof of it – if the groans of the girl were anything to go by. Even so he could not resist delicately lifting the sheet just to make sure. For the first time in his life Delius almost felt intimidated. Still, what he lacked in muscle he more than made up for in finesse, or so he liked to believe.

Thoughts of his latest light of love came to mind. Jelka Rosen was a voluptuous young German painter he had recently met at a party given by his good friend Edvard Munch. He'd first met Toulouse there, too. What a night! It was all happening in the Bohemian quarter in the Paris of 1886, and Delius was right at the heart of it. A counterpoint of distant street cries caressed Jelka's desirable flesh as his mind began to fog over once more, but not before the plaintive memory of the last infatuated student he had casually abandoned reached out to touch him . . . from the depths of the Seine as he floated up towards the light until he broke surface with a gasp and was sitting up in bed wide awake, as a maidservant pulled the curtains admitting the far-off sounds of a city stirring laboriously into life.

Instantly he collapsed back on his pillow with an explosion of relief . . . and a flood of kaleidoscopic images recalling the thrill of last night at the Cirque Fernando with la Belle Equestrienne, the celebrated bareback rider endlessly circling Chocolat and Footit, those irrepressible clowns. And Jelka scoffing marshmallows and Toulouse producing miracles on his sketchpad. Then from the swirling sawdust ring to slow-mo time up in the starlit sky as a spotlit figure on a high wire balanced precariously above the upturned heads, of the breathless crowds below on the Champs-Elysées – as Toulouse speedily caught a moment of suspended time and Delius squeezed Jelka's hand just a little bit tighter.

Then horses hooves, turning wheels, the glittering lights of the black cabs, racing silhouettes against the bright lights of the busy cafés on the far side of the boulevard. Taking their lives in his hands Delius raced his two friends through the heedless traffic, seemingly careless of life and limb. The girl screamed, the midget roared, horses neighed, cabbies cursed, until, safe and sound, the trio collapsed in convenient chairs at a handy café. But the blood of the lovers still raced – even faster than the pencil on the paper of the little genius immortalizing the passing show. And there was dancing – of light in the lovers' eyes, as their mutual exhilaration continued unabated until the memory of the heady afternoon they had spent together on the banks of the Seine induced a more reflective mood. They bathed in its ambience – a lifetime of feeling passed between them as their fingertips made almost imperceptible contact, while Lautrec, equally absorbed in his own world of enchantment, left them to dream on . . . until an urgent voice from the night brought a rude awakening.

The painter made no move, but Delius and Jelka were instantly on their feet and racing to catch up with the well-dressed bearded man making his way swiftly through the seething crowd. His name was William Molard, a composer friend of Delius, more famous for his proximity to a famous neighbour than for his music. The big news was that Gauguin had just got back from Tahiti with his lover, a thirteen-year-old Javanese girl called Annah.

Both Jelka and Delius worshipped Gauguin, and as they hurried through the teeming nightlife of the city that never sleeps they were breathless with excitement at the prospect of paying tribute to their god once more at his notoriously exotic shrine.

Dancing revellers had spilled out of his studio in Montparnasse and on to the balcony as Delius and company entered the courtyard at close on midnight. Racing up the stairs they were confronted on the landing by a whirling dervish in the shape of a dark young girl adorned in nothing but a few bangles, baubles and beads. She was absolutely breathtaking but even more so was the life-size painting of a dusky nude hanging on the wall above the door. Delius's head spun – her pose was provocative, her skin golden, her glance challenging, her body desirable. Memories flared, and suddenly he was back in Florida where a bonfire was raging and a black smile was caught in its bright glow – animated, animal, attainable. Delius, all in white, entered the circle of writhing figures, caught the woman by the wrist and dragged her unresisting into the shadows. The throbbing of his pulse and the beating of the drums raced each other for supremacy as in a haze of alcohol and lust he was sucked into a bacchic maelstrom drenched in waves of sensual melody as if the tendrils of Spanish moss born on a warm breeze in the starlit sky above had found a voice of compelling serenity.

Reluctant to awake from his nocturnal journey into nostalgia Delius forgot all about Gaugin and Jelka and drifted away from the party and only began to surface again as he approached the bright lights of the Champs-Elysées.

Toulouse was still at his table sketching when Delius arrived in time to assist him in draining a bottle of absinthe; after which it was but a short step to fun and games with a couple of tarts at the Moulin Rouge.

Spinning, spinning, everyone and everything was spinning – even the windmill, the giant elephant and eventually the cab bound for their favourite brothel. Then more drinks and words with the madam over accommodation and a hazardous climb up the stairs, assisted by the redoubtable Valentin Desosse, and into their boudoir where they drunkenly approached the king-size bed and slowly, one by one, crashed out.

FIVE

Life's Dance

A SHOT RANG OUT. Uproar! Delius was on his feet instantly. The orchestra stampeded from the pit, the actors took cover. The audience made for every exit in sight. The gangways were blocked. It made front-page news. Edvard Munch read about it next morning . . . and immediately sent a telegram to Delius who, according to the newspaper report, was staying at the Grand Hotel in Christiania just across the street from the theatre. Luckily Delius had escaped with his life despite threats to lynch him.

THERE IS A BOAT LEAVING FOR ASGARDSTRAND AT NOON. IF YOU VALUE YOUR LIFE BE ON IT. I WILL BE WAITING ON THE QUAY WITH A RECEPTION COMMITTEE. AS EVER. E.M.

Ever ready for an excuse to meet up with his dear friend again, the fugitive composer packed his bags, paid the bill, tipped his hat to the venerable troll-like figure of Henrik Ibsen on his way out and left controversy far behind him still bubbling in his wake.

They had first met in Paris a few years ago when Munch was painting a portrait of August Strindberg, yet another of the composer's Bohemian acquaintances. On being introduced, Strindberg said, 'Some say that music should accompany Edvard's pictures if they are to be well and truly under-stood. Are you the man to provide it?'

'I wouldn't presume to try,' said Delius. 'But I am more than happy to sing his praises.' Until this moment he had thought no more about it. Now as the steamer neared the little town, where his friend had recently bought a small house, he seriously entertained the possibility. Memorable paintings dissolved through the calm, milky coastal waters as Delius daydreamed ever southward.

Rue Lafayette, an impressionistic study of a busy, sun-drenched boulevard as seen from the artist's balcony, was a gift, but how to set the top-hatted, tail-coated spectator leaning over the balustrade to music. Now a bird perched on the railing would not present a problem, but a man and a bit of a dandy at that . . . mmm – more up the street of his Teutonic contemporary Richard Strauss perhaps.

Another favourite painting came to mind, *Spring Day on Karl Johan* – a vibrant impressionist study of people reduced to ants swarming up a busy street in Norway's capital city drenched in sunlight – yes, he could certainly evoke a scene like that in music, but as for expressionist works like the *Scream* – no, better send for that neurotic Austrian genius Gustav Mahler.

All the same, Delius found the art of his friend endlessly fascinating, like the man himself, fanatic in his tireless quest for ever new forms of creative expression.

A wispy early evening mist swathed the waiting figures on the quayside in mystery as Delius, leaning on the ship's rail, sought to identify his distinguished friend and the promised welcoming committee.

The thought that the mayor of the little seaside town might possibly be there caused him to search the ranks of the waiting crowd for the glitter of a ceremonial chain of office. No luck, but suddenly an athletic character with a mop of wild red hair and a Vandyke beard was jumping up and down shouting his name. Sure enough, it was Edvard Munch himself accompanied by the welcoming committee in the very desirable shape of two animated young women, also frantically waving. Frederick waved back and breathed a sigh of relief as fears of a formal reception heavy with speech-making were quickly dispelled. Romance was in the air.

Over schnapps in a local tavern Delius assuaged their curiosity about the previous night's riot at the première of a new satirical play by Gunnar Heiberg called *Folkeraadet* (*The People's Parliament*) for which he had written the incidental music. And all the time he was explaining that it was merely a storm in a teacup brought about by his simple parody of the Norwegian National Anthem his attention was concentrated on captivating the charmer sitting opposite playing a furtive game of footsie with him beneath the table. A folksy band tuned up and struck up, and in no time the two couples were on their feet joining in the Friday-night hop-along with the locals.

Their revelry was short lived. Munch suddenly felt unwell and had to be escorted home where he went straight to bed, whereupon the two girls vanished into the night leaving Delius with little choice but to seek out the guest bed-room and sleep it off. Aeons later he awoke to the sound of lapping water and the cry of gulls. Yawning, he heaved himself out of bed, blinked away the remnants of his hangover and gently parted the curtains.

Munch, clothed in nothing but a loincloth, was engrossed in painting a large canvas propped up against a rowing-boat on the nearby beach. Nobody else was about. Delius guessed that it was early. The sun-kissed sea looked inviting. So, acting on impulse, he walked out of the house stark naked, briefly nodded good morning to the artist and plunged headlong into the sea. Munch gave a snort of approval and continued to paint, leaving Delius to float con-tentedly on the gently undulating swell. He used to love swimming, but with increasing age found it more and more of an effort, even though he was only in his mid-thirties. A sudden attack of cramp that shot through his right leg had him gasping in pain. Near panic he splashed his way to the shore. Munch gave him an appraising glance as he approached through the shallows. Tall, slender with an almost feminine grace he captured the artist's attention.

'If it wasn't so chilly I'd ask you to model for me,' he quipped.

As the pain began to subside Delius paused to take in the impressive can-vas his friend was working on. Dancing couples, the men black and sinister, the girls white and vulnerable, whirled in a dreamlike Saturnalia on a dark greensward sweeping down to a beach and the distant sea beyond.

'I can see the very place for me,' said Delius massaging his leg and begin-ning to shiver.

'Where? Bang up against the lone virgin on the left? She's begging for a partner?'

'Far too obvious. I'd much rather be silhouetted against that enormous symbolic phallus rising from the sea.'

Munch smiled. 'Symbolic it may be, but I'm afraid your phallus is nothing but moonlight shining on the midnight sea.'

'I hear music,' said Delius. 'Have you thought of a title yet? I know you set great store by titles.'

'Make a guess.'

'*Life's Dance*,' suggested Delius without a moment's hesitation.

'I always knew you were psychic', said Munch busying himself with palette and brush again.

Delius kissed him on the back of the neck and strode off to the house without another word. Once he was dried and dressed, albeit still unshaven, he threw open his suitcase and unearthed a sheaf of manuscript paper, dug out the stub of a pencil from a coat pocket and started revising his latest symphonic poem that would eventually become known as 'Life's Dance'.

The full score on which he was still working was back at his home in Grez-sur-Loing, but as every note and bar line was fresh in his mind he had no trouble in reworking the development section with which he had never been entirely satisfied. Inspired by his friend's potential masterpiece, Delius reworked the entire passage, not even stopping to eat when Munch popped his head around the door to suggest lunch.

'Glad to be of service,' said his host with a smile when Delius explained the reason.

On and on he worked until the advent of the northern twilight and the sound of not so distant music brought an end to his labours – followed by a good stretch and a walk to the window for a breath of air.

For a moment he thought he was dreaming, for there, down on the greensward by the seashore, was his friend's painting come vividly to life – life-size . . . even down to the full moon caressing the horizon and casting her phallic reflection across the sleeping sea.

On fire, Delius rushed from the house to join the dancing throng. In the middle was Munch himself, dancing with a girl in a red dress Delius did not recognize, while the two women from the day before stood on either side of the painter waiting for partners. Delius grabbed the blonde on the left – a dead ringer for the fair girl in the painting – which did not please the dark one on the right at all. Regardless, he swept his willing partner into the dance oblivious of any music but his own whirling irresistibly around and around in his head. On and on and on they danced in ever-widening musical arcs growing ever wilder until the man and woman found themselves splashing in a racing tide before sinking into a mellow glow of fathomless tranquillity.

SIX

Brigg Fair

*T*HE YEAR 1907 was a momentous one for Delius. At forty-five years of age he was about to get lucky in the land of his birth. Already recognized as a formidable talent in Germany, the land of his fathers, he was still relatively unknown in England. But a meeting with the conductor Thomas Beecham at the première of his Piano Concerto in London was about to change all that. Beecham quickly became a champion of Delius and remained so all his life. He helped to put him on the map and established him there for all time, as his unique recordings testify to this day.

It was a year of great joy and great sorrow. His dear friend Grieg died early in September, but at least there was consolation in the memory of an enjoyable holiday spent together the previous year in Norway where, coincidentally, the seeds of his present happiness were sown. For Percy Grainger had also shared that unforgettable holiday, and it was during this period that he presented Fred with a score of his latest opus, 'Brigg Fair', a brief work scored for tenor solo and unaccompanied voices, for which Grieg himself was largely responsible.

Percy Grainger had originally left his native Australia to further his career as a concert pianist in London, where he soon became fascinated by a number of Norwegian folk settings arranged by Edvard Grieg. And when the two men eventually met the great master was not slow in encouraging Grainger to follow his example in England. Inspired, the young novice set off for Lincolnshire to take down local folksongs from the region's best-known performers. However, the results did not please Grainger, so he returned the following year with an Edison phonograph in the hope of doing better. Accordingly, the accuracy with which Grainger captured the musical variants was greatly enhanced, as his recording of the folk tune 'Brigg Fair' sung by Joseph Taylor, a 72-year-old bailiff, still testifies. And it was from this recording that Grainger fashioned his mini choral masterpiece. Delius, on reading the score, was green with envy.

'If I could have signed my name to this little opus, Percy, I'd die happy,' he remarked to his new friend one day over drinks at a tavern in Trondheim.

'Stand me another pint,' said Grainger, 'and you can have the world rights. The original's been out of copyright for a couple of centuries anyway.'

'You drive a hard bargain,' replied Fred jokingly. 'It's a deal.' And they drank to it.

And, as things turned out, Fred's version remains one of his most popular compositions, while Percy's original unjustifiably gathers dust on the shelves.

Apart from the haunting melody on which both works were based, Delius was very mindful of the lyrics even before he composed a note. These were the words, originally delivered in a wavery voice in a heavy Lincolnshire accent, that Grainger recorded on a wax cylinder – still preserved – in the spring of 1906:

> It was on the fifth of August
> The weather fine and fair
> Unto Brigg Fair I did repair
> For love I was inclined
> I rose up with the lark in the morning
> With my heart so full of glee
> Of thinking there to meet my dear
> Long time I wished to see.
>
> I looked down over my left shoulder
> To see what I could see
> And there I spied my own true love
> Come tripping down to me.

Now Delius had never been to Brigg, miles away in Lincolnshire, but he imagined that it wasn't much different to the local fairs around Bradford which he had been familiar with ever since he could walk.

Ilkley was a firm favourite, but that was associated with his sister Clare, who had always been his own true love in an idealized sort of way, it is true, but the girl who had given him many restless nights in adolescence was undoubtedly 'little' Miss Muffet, a clerk in overseas sales, so called because of her hapless associations with the well-known rhyme and a succession of male suitors forever trying to lure her, unsuccessfully, into their webs. Fred, who occupied the same office, found it difficult to stand up straight whenever she was around, as his feelings for her were all too obvious – thanks to the fashionably tight cut of his trousers. She was just about the only thing connected with the Delius Woollen Works that made life tolerable.

It was August bank holiday, and the boss's son had asked her to join him on an outing to Ibsey fair on the outskirts of Bradford. It was a first, and she was the envy of every girl in the office. Normally she would have enjoyed a lie-in, but for once little Miss Muffet was up with the lark and peering through her window hoping that the sun would soon burn off the early-morning mist. She would risk it and wear her flimsiest dress.

But first a relaxing bath during which she admired her slim legs – then a sprinkle of lavender water and a lingering session with the curling tongs in front of the mirror. As for breakfast, well, she was far too excited to eat, even allowing her tea to get cold as she waited in her best bonnet behind the lace curtains in the front parlour for a first glimpse of her new admirer, while Mum and Dad and two young sisters, all agog, kept her company.

They expected him to appear above the hedge driving a horse and trap. She knew he had one and were rather disappointed when he appeared at the garden gate on foot. Forcing the family to stay where they were – Miss Muffet was rather ashamed of their lowly social status – she answered the front door personally, highly conscious of the impression she was making on the gawpers as her gentleman caller offered her his arm and escorted her down the garden path and out of the gate.

Along the street they strolled, over the turnstile, across the meadow, along by the river, over the bridge and down the valley past grazing cattle, her feet barely touching the ground. She was in heaven, his melodious voice mingling with the sound of bells as a wedding party poured out of the little church accompanied by clouds of confetti and happy laughter. One day she dreamed it might be her throwing a wedding bouquet high in the air for a lucky bridesmaid to pluck out of the blue, blue sky. Did she imagine her handsome escort squeezed her hand a little tighter as the happy couple caught their attention? But almost in the blink of an eye she was aware that Mr Fritz was overcome by melancholy. She didn't know him well enough to ask why but soon worked out the reason as he paused by a fresh tombstone to read the terse inscription:

In Memory of Franz Delius

1879–1880

Safe in the Arms of Jesus

And, as they walked off arm in arm, it seemed that Fritz was moving in time to a funeral march playing silently in his head. And this melancholy mood lasted some little time until the sound of distant music helped to dispel his sadness, which had completely evaporated by the time they were laughing at the dog-faced man at the freak show.

There was much to enjoy at the fair, and he even cajoled her into joining him in a few measures of morris dancing. Then there were the swings and roundabouts and a gypsy fortune-teller – was Mr Fritz the dark stranger she promised? Later came fat, steaming saveloys washed down by a draught or two of Bradford special brew (which, truth to tell, made her head spin) as the village band blazed away and he spun her around and around the wooden dance floor by the light of the setting sun. Thoughtfully, he escorted her home by horse-drawn tram, during which time she must have dozed off, for when they arrived at her stop her head was on his shoulder and he was gently calling her name. All too soon he was knocking at the front door introducing himself to her mother and father and wishing them all a very good night. Pleasantly tired but too excited to sleep, she fantasized about the future, deliriously happy to be caught in his web should he choose to spin one but totally unaware that in a few days' time he would be off to Florida earlier than expected and that she would never see him again.

As for Fritz and his plans for a calculated seduction, they were all forgotten in the fever of preparations for a far more exciting adventure. And it wasn't for close on a quarter of a century that little Miss Muffet occupied Delius's musings once again. The occasion was the composition of 'Brigg Fair', when nostalgic memories of that sunny August day proved to be such a profound inspiration.

As for little Miss Muffet, she died a spinster. Strangely enough 'Brigg Fair' was one of her favourite pieces. One wonders if she ever suspected . . .

SEVEN

Over the Hills and Far Away

A YOUNG MAN IN his early twenties, slight in build with short mousy hair, bespectacled, dressed in a Fair Isle sweater, plus-fours and fell boots sat in the heather on the cliff tops and gazed out over the sun-drenched sea. He was an aspiring composer and he was dreaming, not of fame and celebrity for himself but for the opportunity to help someone who had already achieved that status but who was now completely blind and paralysed. The genius in question was Frederick Delius – a fellow Yorkshireman living in France.

The budding composer, whose name was Eric Fenby, had gleaned these facts while listening to a broadcast of the Delius tone poem Over the Hills and Far Away that he had managed to pick up on his crystal set the previous evening. The announcer had mentioned that locked away in the composer's head were a number of works he was physically incapable of committing to paper. To young Fenby, just on the threshold of a musical career, this news was nothing less than tragic.

And as he pictured the plight of that frustrated composer living in isolation in an obscure village in France he conceived the idea that he might be able to help in bringing those dormant compositions to life. Of course, he would have to leave home, give up his job, say goodbye to all his friends and . . . But, hold on, he hadn't even broached the subject yet – and what if Delius should turn him down? Well, there was only one way to find out and that was to write to the man offering his services – gratis, of course.

News of his decision at home received a stormy reception. The cheek of the boy! Who did he think he was? He was suffering from delusions of grandeur. What truck would a toff like Delius have with a working-class lad from the provinces like him? Not only that, but the contributions from his weekly pay packet would be sorely missed. They weren't made of money, you know. So said his mother and father. His girlfriend Vera was equally put out and let him know in no uncertain terms not to expect her to hang around for him for ever and a day. He wasn't the only fish in the sea.

Actually Fenby wasn't a fish at all; he was an organist at the local cinema where Vera was an usherette. As for his parents, they worked for the town council, so they wouldn't starve; they'd just have to cut back on the booze a bit.

A month later Fenby was on the cross-channel ferry to France. His kind offer had been accepted on behalf of Delius by his wife Jelka, on the understanding that both parties should work at the experiment for a trial period. And, though there would be no financial reward, all Fenby's creature comforts would be well provided for.

Already he was feeling homesick, or was it seasick? Born and bred in the Yorkshire seaside resort of Scarborough he had rarely left the county, let alone the country. And as the white cliffs of Dover were lost in the wake of the little vessel steaming towards the French coast it was the wistful strains of Over the Hills and Far Away that inevitably came to mind. Like his fellow countryman he was going into voluntary exile, bidding adieu to a land Delius's music so potently epitomized.

Two train journeys and a taxi drive later he had already met the portly Mrs Jelka Delius and been shown to his room in a rambling villa in Grez-sur-Loing, a provincial village an hour south of Paris. And, though Fenby had a brief view of the river at the bottom of the garden on arrival, his poky bedsitting-room overlooked the church next door. Well, at least he wouldn't have far to go for daily mass.

He unpacked his suitcase, sat on the bed, sighed and looked about him. A washstand, complete with bowl and basin, took up most of the room, while a selection of gloomy prints and pictures dominating the walls created a sombre mood, unfamiliar and uninviting. A sudden knock on the door made him jump. It was Jelka, in a state of repressed excitement.

'Delius has been carried downstairs. He'll see you now.'

Fenby was slightly taken aback.

'Hurry, hurry,' she exclaimed. 'He's waiting!'

Fenby catapulted to his feet and hastily followed Jelka downstairs and into the living-room. Other than the fact that it was light and spacious Fenby took in no details, focused, as he was, on the frail figure in white enthroned in a high-backed chair sheltered by a large screen open on one side. Reflected in Delius's dark glasses Fenby saw a gauche, embarrassed, bespectacled and oversized schoolboy buttoned up in a grey flannel blazer he had long out-grown . . . Thank goodness Delius couldn't see him.

'Come in, Fenby, come in,' said Delius welcomingly. 'Did you have a pleasant journey?'

Suddenly in the presence of his hero, his god, Fenby was overwhelmed and could only stammer a reply. 'Very pleasant, thank you, sir, though I did have a bit of an upset tummy on the boat.'

A sailor of many summers, Delius ignored this remark. 'I understand you come from Scarborough. Charming place. Used to go there regularly on family holidays. Tell me, do they still have that little German band playing nightly on the prom?'

'Oh no, sir,' replied Fenby, perking up. 'We have a fine local band these days. They play English music now.'

Delius gave Fenby a withering look, in no way tempered by the fact that he was totally blind. 'English music,' he exclaimed with disdain. 'We have no truck with English music here. Tell me, what instrument do you play?'

Dismayed, Fenby nevertheless put on a brave face. 'I play the organ, sir, for the silent films down at the Ritz; mostly Laurel and Hardys.'

'Laurel and Hardys?' exclaimed Delius. 'What on earth are Laurel and Hardys?'

'They're comics, sir,' replied Fenby after an embarrassed pause.

'Comics!' said Delius in disgust. 'Penny dreadfuls, you mean?'

Fenby was speechless.

'They're comedians, Fred,' said Jelka, mindful of the bad impression the visitor was making. 'They work in films. One's fat and one's thin.'

'So I suppose you play farts on the bass notes for the fat one and penny-whistle squeaks on the treble for the thin one,' sneered Delius. 'A regular little Richard Strauss of the cinema, aren't we? Bravo!'

'I'm sorry, sir. I don't quite understand,' said Fenby, totally flummoxed.

'Surely you're familiar with the works of the greatest living German com-poser. He'll set anything to music, from Don Quixote to Sancho Panza – the literary equivalent to your cinematic funny men, my boy. Are you not familiar with Strauss's brilliant orchestral masterpiece Don Quixote?'

'No, sir, I am not,' stammered Fenby. 'But I'm very fond of his Tales of the Vienna Woods.'

'Hah!' scoffed Delius.

Fenby, poor man, had no idea why. But Jelka did. Richard Strauss, the modern German composer of international fame, was not related in any way to his equally famous namesake Johann – the waltz king of Vienna. Surely everyone knew that! She began to have doubts as to the wisdom of this experiment as Delius lapsed into a silence – which no one had the courage to break. In the event it was the composer himself who ended it – with a sharp cry of pain.

'Fetch the Bruder,' screeched Delius, doubled up in agony.

Fenby was undergoing a form of agony himself – rooted to the spot without a clue as to how to behave. Not so Jelka, who was no stranger to her husband's sudden attacks. First she grabbed a striker and gave a handy Chinese gong a single hearty bash, then sprang towards Delius and, having settled him firmly in his chair, gently started to massage the back of his neck. Fenby was still wondering what he could do to help when he was rudely brushed aside by a burly fellow with a beard in knickerbockers who hoisted the composer unceremoniously on to his shoulder and carried him from the room like a sack of potatoes. Jelka followed, fussing around them like a mother hen. Fenby wished fervently he had never been born.

EIGHT

On Hearing the First Cuckoo of Spring

STANDING ALONE IN the garden the morning after his arrival in Grez, Fenby sucked on his pipe and listened. Was that the sound of a cuckoo – the call that invariably conjured up one of the composer's most evocative miniatures?

'You look very pensive, Mr Fenby. Did you sleep well?'

Startled, Fenby spun around. It was Jelka, carrying a small watering-can.

'Good morning, Mrs Delius,' said Fenby. 'Yes, thank you, I slept quite well, considering.'

'Considering what? And please call me Jelka.'

'And please call me Eric.'

'Considering what?'

'Well, it was nothing really,' said Fenby. 'I imagined I heard voices. That's all.'

'I had to call the male nurse at three o'clock to help me lift Delius into another position.'

'Oh, I see. Well, if there's ever anything I can do to help please feel free to ask . . .'

But Jelka had walked off and so did not respond to Fenby's vague offer. Hastily he followed on until he caught up with her watering a tiny newly planted lemon tree.

'Delius is generally brought down at ten-thirty,' said Jelka without further preamble, 'when he will be around for the rest of the day until it is time for his outing, when we will lift him into his wheelchair and push him up the Marlot Road as far as the church . . .' Suddenly she froze as the deep tones of a gong resounded from inside the house. 'That's for you,' said Jelka, a note of panic in her voice. 'One for the man, two for me, three for you.'

Startled, Fenby's only reaction was to take the pipe out of his mouth.

'Hurry, he doesn't like to be kept waiting,' snapped Jelka.

That did it. Fenby sped off.

'Ah, Fenby, read me the headlines of the continental *Daily Mail*,' said Delius by way of a greeting as he heard the lad enter the room.

'Good morning, sir,' said Fenby, picking up the newspaper from a chair next to Delius and taking a seat. Silence ensued until Fenby started to read, 'The Prime Minister is to visit the United States . . .'

'Are my feet touching?' cut in Delius. 'Are my legs straight?'

'Er, yes, sir,' stammered Fenby. 'Er, no . . .'

'Meaning?' boomed Delius.

'Meaning, er, no, your feet are not touching and, yes, your legs are straight, sir.'

'Go on then,' said Delius, irritably. 'Go on, boy.'

Somewhat hot and bothered Fenby continued. 'In his farewell speech to the House of Commons the Prime Minister . . .'

'I'm not in the least interested in what the Premier had to say in Parliament or anywhere else, thank you. Turn on the radio. There's often a concert from Radio Paris at this hour.'

With some relief Fenby jumped to it. And as the familiar strains of a symphonic favourite began to dominate the sound of static he began to smile. 'Ah, Beethoven's Fifth,' he muttered approvingly.

'Beethoven's Fifth – bah!' exclaimed Delius in disgust. 'All scales and arpeggios; long drivelling, note spinning. Go into the fields and listen to the sounds of nature, my boy. Forget the immortals; I finished with them years ago.' And he grimaced in pain. 'This rug is too heavy,' he continued in strangled tones. 'Take it away. Take it off.'

Fenby promptly responded and folded the offending rug away.

Immediately Delius showed signs of relief and became more sanguine. 'I have a little tune in my head I'd like you to take down, Fenby,' he said quietly and calmly. 'You'll find ink, pen and paper over there on the table. Hurry now before I forget it. Are you ready?'

Acting as if he had been stung, Fenby dropped the newspaper and sped across to the table where he took a pen and jabbed it in the inkwell – 'Ready, Delius,' he said, grabbing a piece of paper. But as it turned out he was far from ready for the toneless dirge that followed.

'Der de der, der de der, der de der, hold it. Now did you get that?' snapped Delius.

Stunned, Fenby could only stammer, 'N-no, sir.'

'Very well,' growled Delius. 'We'll try again. Der de der, der de der, der de der, hold it . . . Well?'

By now the half paralysed Fenby was nearly in tears. 'It would help if I knew what key it was in . . .' stammered Fenby.

'Oh, very well then. A minor. Anything else?'

'Fenby was so cowed by now that he could barely speak but managed to blurt out, 'It would help if you called out the notes, sir.'

Delius sighed again wearily and muttered: 'A, B, C, D, D . . .'

But Fenby's fingers were covered with ink by now, in addition to which he had been reduced to a quivering jelly, so . . . nothing.

'Now repeat it,' demanded Delius. 'Repeat it.'

'I'm sorry, sir, I, I . . .' Fenby, at the end of his tether staggered to his feet and ran out of the room – nearly colliding with Jelka in the doorway.

'Fred, Fred, what on earth's the matter?' she demanded, alarmed at Fenby's obvious distress.

'That boy is no good, Jelka. He's too slow,' said Delius bitterly. 'He can't even take down a simple melody.'

As she registered this news Jelka was bitterly disappointed, while Fenby, lingering outside in the passageway, was completely devastated. He had to get out – out of the house and out of the life of this monstrous man. He had to get away . . . now. He started to run, blindly, until, breathless, he stopped at the tiny station where Jelka had met him only yesterday. Such high hopes shattered in less than twenty-four hours. In the distance a train was approaching. He imagined his homecoming; the disgrace, the sneers. It would be so easy just to tumble on to the line; then oblivion – no more cares, no more worries.

It was much closer now – then Jelka came to mind; not Delius but Jelka. She believed in him; she depended on him. He just could not abandon her. The train roared past leaving him physically unscathed.

'You've been crying,' observed Jelka bluntly when she saw him later in the day.

'I got a smut in my eye.'

'A smut?' queried Jelka. 'We haven't had a fire in weeks.'

'I was at the station,' said Fenby, wishing he hadn't spoken.

Jelka, bless her, deemed it wisest to take the bull by the horns. 'You must stand up to him, Eric, and you must find a way of working together. Now please make a practical suggestion as to how.'

Put on the spot, Fenby stated the obvious. 'Well, you can't do much without a piano.'

'We have two. Take your pick.'

'Which is the best?'

'The one in the upstairs music room. It's a Steinway.'

'That'll do.'

'What else?'

'I'd like Delius delivered there every single day whenever's the best time for him.'

'Health permitting that would be first thing after lunch. A few glasses of wine often works wonders.'

'Then I'll have a go, Jelka,' said Fenby with new-found fortitude.

Thus started five years' hard labour.

NINE

Song of Summer

'*N*ow, ERIC, I want you to imagine that you are sitting in the heather on top of the cliffs at Filey overlooking the sea on a breezy summer's day.'

Delius and Fenby were about to start work on a new tone poem, and the old man was putting his amanuensis in the picture. And, though they were sitting in the music room at Grez, far from that picturesque spot on the Yorkshire coast, Eric knew the location very well so had no problem whatsoever in calling it to mind.

Delius went on to explain that as a basis for the new work he intended to incorporate some of the ideas in an orchestral work he had written back in 1918. It was entitled A Poem of Life and Love and had never been performed. This came as no surprise to Eric who had studied the score and found much of it generally lacking in taste, despite isolated moments of pure inspiration. It was ripe for reworking. And so for many months, with Eric at the piano and Delius seated by his side, they fought to give life to something of real potential that might well have remained stillborn. It was a battle of wills, with Delius calling out the notes and instrumentation and Eric illustrating them on the piano and occasionally suggesting alternatives and thoughts of his own.

Sometimes they spurred each other on; sometimes they went at it hammer and tongs, while Jelka, potting geranium cuttings beneath their window, would smile to herself and thank providence for a collaboration made in heaven. For Eric Fenby had succeeded against all odds where others, of far greater technical ability, had failed. Both Percy Grainger and Philip Heseltine, talented composers in their own right, were temperamentally incapable of collaborating with such a short-tempered and headstrong character as Delius, try as they might, though they undoubtedly loved the man and respected his genius.

Jelka had also tried to help from time to time with results that put the marriage in jeopardy and threatened her sanity. God knows what Fenby must be feeling. He had put up with it for close on two years. How much longer would he be able to stand the strain of Delius's wild mood swings, not to mention the lack of companionship of people his own age? Sometimes Jelka wished poor Eric would have a fling with Colette, the maid. She was a pretty little thing. And had he been more active Fred would almost certainly have made a pass at her himself. One should be thankful for small mercies. Yes, at last the collaboration was working – the sounds that drifted down to Jelka from the music room seemed very promising.

It was a promise that was fulfilled to her complete satisfaction eighteen months later by Sir Henry Wood conducting an outstanding broadcast performance from the Royal Albert Hall in London. Jelka and Delius heard it on their recently purchased wireless set at their home in Grez.

'Oh, Jelka, Jelka,' groaned the exasperated composer as the conductor walked on to the platform to much applause. 'If you are going to bellow like a carthorse kindly remove yourself from earshot or I won't be able to hear a blessed thing.'

'Right, Fred, of course,' Jelka panted as she hurried to the other side of the room. 'Right away.'

The reason for her stentorian breathing Jelka kept to herself. Fred wouldn't be interested. She had run around the village begging and pleading with all those in possession of generators and electrical appliances kindly to turn them off 'pour une demi-heure, s'il vous plaît', as the interference they caused could result in the music being distorted out of all recognition. And more than one of the potential offenders had needed not only frantic persuasion but also bribes and promises.

But Jelka's persistence paid off – for most of the time the transmission was nigh on perfect. And so was the performance itself, mainly owing to the dedication of Fenby who was attending the concert in person. Not only had he supervised the printing of the parts, he had also gone through every note of the score with the conductor, in addition to supervising all the rehearsals and coaching some of the soloists.

And, as the conductor raised his baton, between Jelka, Delius and Fenby there was a profound communion of souls – even if the journeys they were about to undertake were completely at variance.

Jelka, seated in a corner and doing her best not to breathe, found the experience almost unbearably poignant. It carried her back to the year 1918 and happy days spent with Delius at Biarritz where he was hard at work on a new composition entitled 'A Poem of Life and Love'. After a passage of close on thirteen years Jelka recognized a theme she had first heard on the piano now clothed in exquisite orchestral garb that caused her pulse to race. Happy days – that was the time when Delius was still proficient at the keyboard and still able to make love and bask on the sand and swim in the sea.

Also her former best friend and rival for Delius's affections was no longer on the scene, and the war had put paid to his frequent trips to the fleshpots of Paris. They had never been happier. But it was too good to last. On their return to Grez they discovered that the French troops who had requisitioned their home had left it a complete shambles and quite uninhabitable. So while reconstruction was under way they sought refuge in London where Delius's health began to deteriorate.

Everything was rationed. There was a shortage of food and a shortage of fuel. Their north-London flat was cold and damp, and there was the endless fog to contend with. As for the social scene, Delius found it superficial and decadent.

His health declined and he was further depressed by news of the death on the Western Front of his favourite sister's only son. The love-making came to an end.

Jelka's musings were cut short when she spotted Delius frowning: someone had switched on a generator with the result that a delectable flute solo was drowned in static. But that was not entirely responsible for his pained expression – his entire body was aching like hell. But what he had just heard gave him hope for the future, even though time was running out. What next? Another work from the past came to mind: *Margot le Rouge* – a short opera about a heartless prostitute – which had never been performed. That, too, might be ripe for resurrection. He would start on it just as soon as Fenby got back from England.

And Fenby, what was he going through, sitting alone in a box high above the orchestra in the Albert Hall? Well, he had eyes only for the principal flautist, an attractive blonde in her mid-twenties, around the same age as himself. Acting on the conductor's advice, he had helped her with the phrasing of her solos and in doing so had fallen completely under her spell. So far in his short life he hadn't much luck with the opposite sex. This was down partly to the restraints of his religion (he was a devout Catholic), partly to his studious appearance and partly to his acute shyness. But, despite himself, the sheer evocative power of the music transported him from his immediate surroundings to memories of summer days, roaming the clifftops in Yorkshire and thrilling to the sound of the waves breaking on the rocks below as the glorious lower strings slowly rose and fell and a filigree figure on the flute conjured up the image of a seagull gliding by. Then, as the music became more sensual and grew towards a climax, he visualized a couple lying in the heather making love – which had him blushing and wondering whether Delius had ever consciously set the sex act to music. The fact that the composer used to holiday there at the seaside in the days of his youth made it highly likely. For, to judge from photographs, he had been a smashing-looking young man – a bit of a ladykiller in fact.

The applause snapped him out of it. The conductor took his bow and turned to the pretty blonde flautist, encouraging her to do likewise. She did so and smiled up in Fenby's direction. He was in heaven.

TEN

Song on the High Hills

'H E'S THROWING A tennis ball over the house,' exclaimed Jelka, as she straightened up from her weeding. Fenby, sitting near by close to Delius, paused in his recounting of a Sherlock Holmes murder mystery to take in the unusual sight of a small ball high in the summer sky.

'Now he'll run through the house and catch it at the other side,' said Delius, suddenly excited as a virile red-headed man dashed inside. Fenby blinked in surprise, but before he had time to blink again the young man had emerged from the house triumphantly holding the ball – which he deftly pocketed before grabbing hold of Delius's wheelchair and propelling him down the garden path at breakneck speed. That was surprising enough, but even more so was the whoop of joy from Delius that almost made Fenby jump out of his skin.

With furrowed brow he turned to Jelka for enlightenment.

'That's Percy Grainger,' she said. 'Sometimes he composes.' And that was Fenby's introduction to Australia's greatest composer.

After dinner Fenby and Grainger played a two-piano version by the latter of Delius's 'Song of the High Hills' as the old couple listened entranced. Jelka was actually weeping.

Afterwards, as they sipped champagne in honour of Percy's inspired achievement, the old friends reminisced over happy days in Norway, including the memorable climb they had all enjoyed just before Delius lost his sight. But, reading between the lines, Fenby soon deduced that, though Delius undoubtedly relished the experience, both Percy and Jelka – especially Jelka – simply had to endure it. With the help of a burly Norwegian guide they had strapped Fred to a chair, lashed it to a couple of poles and lugged him all the way up to the top of a hill in a freezing mist, which miraculously cleared to reveal a most glorious sunset.

'It was bloody agony,' Grainger confided to Fenby the next day over a carafe of wine in the local café.

So that's why there were tears in her eyes, thought Fenby.

'Poor Jelka was completely knackered. She was in front sharing the strain with the mountain guide, while I took the weight at the rear,' Grainger went on. 'And despite the fact Delius was no more than a bag of bones it all but ruptured me. No, I tell a lie, double-ruptured me. I had a pole in each hand, you see. And not one word of thanks, only "Steady on there, you're making me seasick." I could have murdered the bastard. Poor Jelka, how she's put up with him all these years I really don't know. I can only imagine she must be into masochism like the rest of us.'

'Into what?' questioned Fenby, not quite able to believe his ears.

'Into masochism. You know, flagellation and so forth.'

'No, I certainly do not know! Who do you think I am?'

'You're a Catholic, aren't you,' said Grainger sharply.

'Yes, and proud of it,' replied Fenby, uncharacteristically raising his voice.

'I thought pride was a Catholic sin,' said Grainger, calmly taking a sip of wine. 'Keep your shirt on, cobber. It was you Catholics who dreamed up the entire notion of flagellation in the first place. And why? Could it be to demonstrate that one is genuinely willing to suffer for one's faith? And to prove one is willing to endure pain for a high ideal. Aren't you willing to suffer the scourge of Fred's tongue in exchange for the exquisite joy of a new creation? If that isn't masochism, what is?'

'What first brought you and Delius together,' ventured Fenby, desperately trying to change the subject.

Unsuccessfully, as it turned out, for Grainger answered, with a hint of mirth, 'Sex!'

Whereupon Fenby attempted to conceal his discomfort by laboriously filling and lighting his pipe.

'Here you see the typical Englishman,' exclaimed Grainger, suddenly addressing a nosy peasant at a nearby table. 'One mention of the word sex and he disappears behind a smoke-screen.' But Grainger's remark fell on deaf ears, as the peasant could not understand him. Nevertheless Fenby blushed to the roots of his being and fell into an agony of silence.

Unrelenting, Grainger went on, 'Sex, love, pain, they're all closely related, Fenby – nothing to be ashamed of. The only contact I ever had with my mother was through the stinging palm of her hand when I was a naughty boy. She never once gave me a hug or kissed me good night; not through indifference, mind you, but through concern – concern that she might infect me with the disease she had contracted from my father. For despite having a beautiful and loving wife he had a weakness for contaminated whores. My mother's name was Rose. I saw her wither before my eyes. How I longed for her to touch me. The only way to achieve this was to annoy her, drive her to distraction so that she would eventually lose control and thrash me. That was true ecstasy, Fenby, believe me. That is why I am an unashamed masochist. Fred, now, is the exact opposite. He likes dishing it out. I imagine you've had to put up with a bit of stick from time to time yourself. He used to have a strong right arm when first we met and many's the time I enjoyed the force of it whenever he gave me a good flogging. Disgusting you, am I, Fenby?' Grainger asked, registering the other's increasing disquiet. 'You find it increasingly difficult to equate a man's secret life with his creative life. Did you know that Mozart, for instance, used to eat his own shit?'

That was it! Trembling, Fenby rose to his feet and stormed out. The café had become unbearably claustrophobic. Outside he gulped in quantities of fresh air and set off briskly for the river, unaware that Grainger was following him. He finally caught up with Fenby as he was leaning over the stone parapet of the bridge gazing into the weedy waters of the river Loing.

'Thinking of ending it all,' joked Grainger, hopping up on to the narrow parapet and balancing precariously on one leg reminiscent of Eros at Piccadilly Circus.

'Suicide is yet another Catholic sin,' Fenby blurted out in a rage. 'It's not an option.'

'Ah, found your tongue at last,' laughed Grainger, jumping down beside him. 'I know what you're really thinking – you're in despair over the truth of the irrational. How can such godawful shits write such heavenly music? Am I right?' Once again Fenby lapsed into silence. 'Come on,' urged Grainger. 'Am I?' Still no reply. 'Now admit it,' Grainger persisted. 'Take "Song of the High Hills". Whenever you hear it your spirit soars . . . right?'

Reluctantly Fenby nodded.

'Thank you. The mute speaks.' No response but Grainger persisted. 'So we are both agreed that Fred not only touched the heights with that score, not only reached the peaks, but soared high above them – out of sight to the likes of lesser mortals like you and me. Right?'

'Right,' muttered Fenby, biting on to the pipe he had lit once more.

'But do you love it any less when I tell you that it was on the very hills that inspired this sublime masterpiece that Fred fucked a twelve-year-girl who later died in childbirth? Does that fact detract in any way from the supreme grandeur of his musical achievement.'

Fenby went white. 'That can't be true,' he gasped. 'You're making it up.'

'Maybe it's true, maybe it's just a vicious slur. But so far as the value of the music and the music alone is concerned, does it really matter . . . either way?' And he turned and ran off, knowing full well that even if he'd waited for a month of Sundays Fenby would still be stuck for an answer.

ELEVEN

Summer Night on the River

PROPPED UP ON pillows he was drifting and dreaming. His eyes were closed and, as long as they remained so, he could not tell if he was blind or not. It didn't matter; the familiar images flowed steadily through his mind like a well-loved moving picture constantly dissolving from one memory to another.

There was Jelka at her easel in the garden framed in a bower of roses, viewed through a screen of flickering irises and a rainbow of incandescent dragonflies as he glided slowly by.

Then there was the skeletal figure of a blind man in a straw hat and summer whites sitting in a wheelchair with a naked woman kneeling at his feet engaged in oral sex, a scene that became gradually obscured by a frantic curtain of gnats rising from the oily surface of the water. Women, women, women . . .

And the undulating water-weed beckoning from the depths recalling songs of the sirens who had lured him into the waters of every fashionable spa in Europe: Topsy, Kate, Bertha, Bella, Ingrid, Ida. The three M's – Margot, Marcelle, Maud – and Valentine and Zara were just some of the women who might have been guilty, while Baden-Baden, Bad Oeynhausen, Mammern, Biarritz, Wiesbaden, Dresden and Lauvaasen were just some of the sanatoriums to which they had condemned him.

Blondes, redheads, brunettes, black, white and khaki, he'd enjoyed them all and remembered them all as he soaked his way through every fashionable watering-hole on the entire continent: hot water, cold water, still water, rushing water, mineral water, clear water, cloudy water, rose water, rain water, salt water – any kind of water that might buoy up the hope of a cure. Or at least hope of prising out of his paralysed body those unheard melodies locked in his tortured mind. The only water he had no truck with was holy water – Devil's brew! And as he drifted on, waiting for the bump that would herald the fatal shock of his arrival on the other side, he was conscious of another presence close at hand.

'Is that you, Jelka?' he asked.

'No, Delius, it's Eric,' came the reply. 'Would you like me to wake her?'

'What time is it?'

'It's nearly three o'clock.'

'Morning or night-time? I'm not clairvoyant, you know.'

'Sorry, Delius,' said Eric apologetically. 'It's night-time. Do you want me to wake Jelka? She said that if you needed . . .'

'No, no, no,' cut in Delius sharply, before adding with a chuckle. 'Let sleeping dogs lie.'

'Can I get you anything?'

'There's a crease in my nightshirt – it's hurting my arm. Straighten it out.'

'Which arm?' asked Eric nervously.

'Isn't it obvious? The left arm, the left arm.'

Eric did as he was told.

Delius screamed. 'I'm not a punch bag, boy,' he bellowed. 'You're supposed to be a pianist not a pugilist. Where's that delicate touch you take such pride in?'

Eric tried again. 'There, Delius, is that better?'

No answer, but Eric reacted in alarm as he saw Delius's lips drawn back in a rictus grin as his entire body convulsed in an arc of pain culminating in a total collapse over the side of the bed. If Delius had been in the drifting boat of his imagination the fingers of the long-suffering man would have trailed in the water – seeking to caress the beckoning hair of those heartless sirens. And as if thinking made it, so one bold harpy reached up and, taking him by the wrist, planted a kiss as cold as steel just above his heart. In reality a doctor had entered the room, taken his pulse and applied a stethoscope to the stricken man's chest. That imagined kiss was the last thing he ever felt.

'Il est mort,' said the physician.

Eric gently closed the lids on the eyes as sightless in death as they had been in the declining years of the musician's life. He made the sign of the cross on Delius's forehead with holy water.

The river froze over.

It was Sunday 10 June 1934.

TWELVE

Requiem

FENBY WAS IN the garden picking roses. He was very selective and chose only those flowers in full bloom that would give up their fragile petals without a fight. Jelka wanted them to sprinkle over the body.

Delius had died the night before, and the young man was still in shock; not so much at the death itself as the cause of it – which had been revealed to him only a short while before.

The composer had been in a bad way, and despite the fact that it was three in the morning the doctor had been called. A routine examination was followed by a shot of morphine, after which the physician took Fenby aside and informed him that his friend was dying.

Fenby had been vehement. 'Nonsense! Delius has suffered these attacks for years,' he protested. 'He's as tough as old boots. He'll pull through again, you'll see.'

Unfamiliar with the English idiom and with no time to waste on niceties, the doctor had bluntly replied, 'Monsieur Delius is terminally ill. He is in the advanced stages of syphilis. There is no hope for him, no hope at all.' And with that he was gone.

Fenby had been stunned, rooted to the spot. What a fool he'd been! For not once during his five-year sentence had he suspected the truth. Unwittingly, he'd been part of a great conspiracy. He felt angry, betrayed. He had often discussed Delius's plight both with visitors at Grez and interested parties back in England. Kidney trouble, nervous disorders, Delius was constantly under diagnosis and constantly seeking a cure for what ailed him. Obviously there was no cure. All those treatments – from hypnotism to hydrotherapy – were a sham, a game of charades. As Fenby was to discover later there was only one treatment for a dose of the pox and that was a dose of mercury, which frequently caused more pain than it was prescribed to assuage. A once meaningless phrase from the past came vividly to mind: 'A moment with Venus, a lifetime with Mercury.'

What a fool he had been. How naïve. And what of Delius's friends Barjansky, Grainger, Beecham, Heseltine – were they all in the know? Was he alone the odd man out? Did they all laugh behind his back – at him, the stupid little virgin from Scarborough? Yet, come to think of it, all the signs were there, right enough. Unguarded moments between husband and wife, innuendo and anecdotes from inebriated visitors and even occasional local gossip. God, how blind he'd been, blind as a bat.

Delius had deceived him – it cut to the bone. And to think that he had sacrificed his own career to dedicate himself to an old reprobate who had brought his disability on himself. Serve him right if he had never written another note. And what about poor Jelka? Delius had deceived her, too. Had he infected her? Perish the thought. Either way, she had certainly been made to suffer because of his sins.

After Delius died Fenby walked to the church to pray for him. It was the first time he had set foot there since the first week of his arrival. Delius had forbidden it. Fenby remembered the occasion well.

They had been listening to a programme of recorded music from Radio Paris when a piece of Gregorian chant was announced to be sung by the monks of Quorr Abbey.

'May I turn up the volume, please, sir?' asked Fenby. 'It's a little bit quiet, don't you think?'

As he waited for a reply Fenby was surprised to see a look of alarm from Jelka, who turned to him and shook her head violently.

Delius replied in the iciest of tones. 'To my way of thinking, it's not quiet enough. Kindly kill it, will you please, Jelka, and put us out of our misery. I take it you are an advocate of religious music, Fenby.'

Another warning look from Jelka told Fenby that he was on dangerous ground. Nevertheless he unwisely spoke his mind. 'Not all of it, sir, not by any means, but I really do admire Haydn's *The Creation* – "And God Created Great Whales –"'

'God,' cut in Delius, disparagingly. 'God. I don't know him, and don't talk to me of oratorios. Elgar wasted most of his life writing long-winded oratorios. It was the penalty he paid for his English upbringing. Mendelssohn gave the

British public exactly what it wanted – 'Oh Rest in the Lord' – and Parry would have set the entire Bible to music had he lived long enough. English music will never be any good until they get rid of Jesus.' Here he stopped, breathless, exhausted.

Jelka was the first to speak. 'Mr Fenby tells me he will be attending daily mass, Fred.' This was patently not a wise revelation but one that Jelka felt was necessary. Better to break the news this way rather than for him to learn it from a village gossip.

'Well, if you must go to mass use the church in the next village,' Delius commanded. 'After all these years of abstention we've no wish to set a bad example. And if you want to amount to anything in the world of music, Fenby, the first thing you must do is get rid of those Christian blinkers.'

All this passed quickly through Fenby's mind as he knelt to pray in the church that Delius had denied him for all those intervening years. 'How to begin? Please, Lord, forgive him his trespasses, forgive him his blindness to your divine benefice, forgive . . .' Here he stopped as a heretical thought crossed his mind. Perhaps the boot should be on the other foot. Perhaps Almighty God should be asking forgiveness of Delius for striking him down with such a terrible affliction in the first place. Would a truly loving God wish such a dreadful plague on the heads of his children whose only crime was desire for a surfeit of ecstasy?

But even if Delius was guilty of transgressing the laws of God surely the poor man had atoned for his sins with every note of music he had written ever since. Hadn't God punished him enough? Fenby checked himself, blamed himself for unwittingly playing the Devil's advocate. How the old agnostic would have laughed if he could see him now. For Delius there was no Devil and no God either but simply a force of nature that ruled the universe with an enigmatical set of precepts aeons beyond human understanding. And, as Delius had often pointed out, since the beginning of time more people had been killed in the name of God than by any act of nature. Delius was a pantheist who venerated human existence while deploring the carnage of war and particularly the senseless massacre of young talent. In fact, he had written a requiem dedicated to the memory of young artists killed in the Great War. In close on twenty years it had received only one performance. It wasn't hard to see why. Firmly pagan, it mocked religion and extolled the eternal return of springtime. But in his philosophy there was no return for man, no resurrection, just the chance of something better, the chance to leave behind a gift that could be treasured by generations to come. Fenby pulled himself up. He was beginning to indulge in heretical beliefs. A moment later he was in a confessional reciting his sins and asking forgiveness. As a penance he was told to get to his knees and say three Our Fathers and three Hail Marys, after which he felt very much better.

THIRTEEN

The Walk to the Paradise Gardens

ELIUS WAS DRESSED in his summer whites, but, despite Herculean
endeavours, Fenby had been unable to force his white canvas shoes
on to his bony feet, so he had to make do with carpet slippers. This
had the effect of making him look quite undignified – not that he minded, poor
man, he was dead and as cold as mutton. He was laid out on the *chaise-longue*
in the music room, awaiting the arrival of the undertaker. Fenby was
exhausted. He had never laid anyone out before and never touched a human
body in such an intimate way – and fervently hoped he would never have
occasion to do so again.

He had had no option – the two servants had flatly refused, and Jelka, confined to her wheelchair, was worse than useless. Fenby had never seen a body
in the advanced stages of syphilis before, especially with the diseased member
triumphantly rampant in its state of rigor mortis and attired in royal purple.
Even now it proclaimed its ascendancy over life as it strained against the dead
man's buttoned fly – there for all to see. What to do? Jelka would be putting in
an appearance soon, causing Fenby frantically to search for a way to spare her
blushes. He tried to scatter a few rose petals on the offending mound, but this
only succeeded in turning it into a miniature Mont Blanc, so he hastily
removed them.

And he was seriously considering rolling the poor man over on to his stomach
when Jelka was wheeled into the room by the maidservant. The latter, poor girl,
was mesmerized by the rampant Pantheism of the cadaver and couldn't tear
her eyes away. She must have thought it had a life of its own, Fenby surmised,
while Jelka seemed quite oblivious.

'It's eight o'clock in England,' she exclaimed. 'Turn on the Home Service,
Eric. We may be just in time.'

Fenby nodded, sped over to the wireless, switched on and tuned in – as through the static came the plummy voice of a BBC announcer, '. . . passed away at three a.m. today at his home in France. Born in Bradford, Yorkshire, in 1862 Delius spent most of his life abroad and found his chief inspiration in the realms of nature in which, like Wordsworth before him, he heard the still, sad music of humanity. After 1918 he became subject to an illness which rendered him blind and paralysed. But despite these incredible handicaps he was still able to compose until only a few months before his death. In this he was aided by the dedication of his young amanuensis Eric Fenby. Here is a fragment of one of his most sublime works, The Walk to the Paradise Gardens.'

There followed a few moments of that sublime music until it was drowned in static as a generator started up in the house next door. Thank God Delius isn't around to hear it, thought Fenby. He'd have turned the air quite blue.

FOURTEEN

Double Concerto

*T*HE HARRISON SISTERS, May and Beatrice, had just left and would never set foot in Grez again – thank God. Bad thought – leave God out of it. They had venerated Delius like a God and vice versa. From the very first moment Delius had heard them play the Brahms Concerto for Violin and Cello he had worshipped at their shrine. Poor man, he had always been a pushover for a pretty face, even in a Greek dress, and that's how he had first seen them playing at that concert in Manchester during the war. Afterwards at the champagne reception in their honour he had been all over them. It was embarrassing. Two glasses of bubbly and he was promising to write a concerto especially for them, he, who after the failure of his Piano Concerto, swore he'd never write another concerto ever again. Jelka was livid!

The war had mercifully put an end to his philandering in Paris, and just when it seemed he might settle down at last he became besotted by a couple of flashy twenty-year-olds. Heck! Their hair was even styled à la Grecque. They all but ignored Jelka, those chattering magpies, even though Fred had introduced her as his 'artistic wife' – though almost in passing, it has to be said. However, the ebullient girls were superficially more than polite to her, and when Fred suggested a musical collaboration between composer and soloists they not only proposed they work together in their gorgeous music room but invited Jelka along as well – to immortalize the momentous event on canvas. An invitation Jelka refused in the same spirit as that in which it was offered.

Fred had never seemed happier – which made the succession of lonely days spent in their damp north-London flat all the more difficult for her to bear. She gave up cooking supper for him, because the food was invariably spoiled before he got home of an evening. And there were nights when he never came home at all. And as was her habit, cultivated stoically over the years, she never asked why. She knew that in this cosy little *menage à trois* there was no place for her. Eventually the wretched piece was finished and Fred had no further excuse to hang around their skirts. So it was with a great sense of relief that she organized the packing and the trip back to Grez. Sanctuary at last, at least for a while.

But on 21 February 1920, at the Queen's Hall in London, it started all over again. The occasion was the world première of the Double Concerto for Violin and Cello with May and Beatrice as soloists under the masterful baton of Sir Henry J. Wood.

And, if the following entry in her secret diary is to be believed. Jelka found the performance almost indecent:

> To say it was erotic would be an understatement, but propriety demands restraint, though I am ashamed to say that the language of the gutter would best describe the unbidden images that sprang to mind as those brazen performers revealed their sordid secrets for all to witness. I looked about me prepared to see a shocked audience hiding their blushes. Unbelievably, the only one affected appeared to be me – my face was on fire, and I thanked God I was wearing a heavy veil. I glanced at Delius, sitting by my side. His eyes were closed and he was wearing an enigmatic smile, which seemed to grow ever more lewd the longer I gazed. It became so loathsome to me that I was driven to divert my gaze back to the platform only to become mesmerized by the manner in which Beatrice was manhandling that loathsome instrument between her legs. It was obscene. I closed my eyes tight shut. Tears were running down my face. I imagined rivulets of mascara spoiling my powdered cheeks. Suddenly Fred gripped my hand in his. This I found nearly unbearable. I almost choked . . . and started to cough uncontrollably. I tore away my hand to cover my mouth . . . but the coughing wouldn't stop. I prayed desperately until it was finally drowned in a roar of rapturous applause. Fred told me later that he excused my absence from the reception that followed by saying that I was moved to tears and had retired to repair the damage – always the perfect gentleman.

What Jelka didn't learn until much later was that Fred had been so impressed with the girls, particularly Beatrice, that he promised her a concerto of her very own . . . which meant they'd be spending even more time together.

However, Fred kept Jelka in the dark about all that, and it wasn't until the wretched girl turned up at Grez unannounced to discuss the matter further that Jelka had the first inkling. In the event she was furious but, as usual, had no option but to bite her tongue – what was left of it.

The following Easter found the Deliuses back in London in a flat at Swiss Cottage, though Fred spent most of his days at Thames Ditton in Surrey where the Harrisons had rented an idyllic farmhouse. Jelka was invited, too, but soon got tired of playing gooseberry and took to traipsing around the London galleries instead. However, acting on an impulse she turned up unexpectedly one day to find the pair hand in hand sunbathing on the lawn – absorbing the heartbeat of mother earth which, they said, they were studying as a possible metronome indication for the first movement. Staying just long enough to choke down a snack of cheese and pickles and knock off a quick sketch of a pet donkey, Jelka wished them 'bon chance' and caught the next train back to town – wondering on the way just how they would go about seeking inspiration for the slow movement. Too distressing! She put further speculation out of her mind.

After what seemed like an age they were back home in Grez. but even there Baba, as Fred called her, was still very much around in spirit, for Fred never missed a broadcast in which she was a featured soloist. Once when the BBC transmitted a programme from her garden in Surrey in which she accompanied a nightingale on the cello he was visibly moved to tears. It was shameful.

Jelka's only consolation was that the première of the concerto took place in Vienna with her talented friend Barjansky as soloist. But that never stopped the bitch from turning up on the doorstep with an accompanist to give Fred a private performance – which once again moved him to tears. It was embarrassing. And to add further insult to injury she also brought her mother and kid sister, Margaret, who not only played the Violin Concerto but also two sonatas as well. How poor Jelka, as a reluctant member of the audience, suffered. It was agony. Her one consolation was that by this time Delius was blind and partially paralysed; though that would not prevent him giving them a good grope should he get half a chance, she surmised.

But even though he was dead now they still had dominion over him. As she heard the taxi drive them off to the station for the last time she wondered why she had agreed to Fred being disinterred from the graveyard next door, where he had been buried for close on a year, and transported to England to be reburied close to the Harrisons' home in Surrey. Even so she consented to be buried with him. She loved him, you see.

FIFTEEN

In a Summer Garden

To My Wife Jelka:
All are my blooms, and all sweet blooms of love
To thee I gave while spring and summer sang

*I*T WAS NO secret. There it was for all to see right at the top of the score. His wedding gift to her – a magical distillation in the form of a miniature tone poem, lasting a little less than a quarter of an hour, acknowledging her years of toil and dedication spent in transforming a barren plot of land between their house and the river into a Garden of Eden.

The young man standing in the darkened room with Jelka and her nurse was fully aware of this as he wound up the portable gramophone he had lugged along with him, together with a heavy box of shellac records.

He was a BBC sound engineer who had been ordered by none other than the Director General himself to record the highlights of the funeral service of Frederick Delius, the lady's husband. After which he was instructed to visit the nursing home in Surrey where she lay seriously ill with cancer and play back his efforts. And that was the full extent of his brief. But acting on impulse he had also brought along a selection of Delius's commercial recordings in the hope that they might cheer her up a bit.

However, the response of the dying woman to the young man's efforts to catch something of the mournful flavour of the graveside eulogy dominated by the squawking of a blackbird appeared to be extremely non-committal to say the least.

Somewhat discouraged, the young man quietly asked the nurse whether she thought Mrs Delius might like to hear some of her husband's music. The nurse nodded her acquiescence, and moments later there was a click and a hiss as the heavy pick-up was gently lowered on to the spinning record. Then followed an emasculated version of the composer's immortal sound picture.

Imagine a heavenly garden shimmering in the heat of summer, drenched in the perfume of countless flowers playing host to a dancing cloud of butterflies, while in the shadow of a weeping willow overhanging the lazy waters of the river is moored a punt with two reclining figures. Birdsong fills the air.

Yes, all that was there in the music, various aspects of which Jelka had often reflected in her evocative impressionist paintings. And though the young man had no knowledge of this he may well have guessed as much.

But what of Jelka? What was going through her mind as with every reluctant breath she edged ever closer towards death's open door? Her body motionless, her face expressionless, her eyes sightless beneath heavily hooded lids.

She has the look of a peasant, thought the young man from the BBC, who had never seen a peasant in his life. And he was not alone in making that observation. Delius had been of the same opinion and was not above drawing his wife's attention to the fact on those frequent occasions she inadvertently committed some minor transgression.

That hurt. Jelka was an artist. It was her burning desire to become a painter that had brought her to Paris to study at the Académie Colarossi in the first place. Of course, she could never compete with the grand names Fred numbered among his numerous friends and acquaintances, but if her oil paintings were far from being great works of art then her garden most certainly was. Some said that Delius was more in love with her garden than the lady herself. He practically lived in it. It was a continuous visual and sensual delight, year in, year out, a constant inspiration. And as the vibrant ever-changing colours became ever more pastel and impressionistic as his sight slowly clouded over, so the scents and sounds associated with them grew ever more evocative and sensual. Even the young man from the BBC got a whiff of it and began to wonder whether it was having a similar effect on the old woman lying comatose between the crisp white sheets.

He found himself wondering whether husband and wife had ever made love in that riverside earthly paradise enshrined, albeit far from ideally, on that revolving disc. Silly thought. They must have; it was there in the music. He had never heard anything so seductive. It made Scriabin's Poem of Ecstasy sound like plain chant in a convent. And he wasn't far off the mark. Delius had made love in that garden, and, yes, there it was in the music – but never to his wife. And those two people almost hidden in the punt under the trees; could they be Delius and Ida Gerhardi – Jelka's best friend? Or was the mystery woman, that attractive nude model simply known as Marcelle? Yes, it certainly was Delius, but it certainly wasn't Jelka.

Swish, swish, swish. The needle swished in the run-off groove, and clunk went the auto-brake. The BBC man wondered if he should play something else. Summer Night on the River perhaps.

'I think you should go now,' said the nurse.

He nodded, packed up his things and took a final look at the dying woman. Her eyelashes seemed a little moist. The nurse made no attempt to dab them dry. Burdened by his equipment, the BBC man crept softly across the polished wooden floor towards the door. His boots squeaked. It was the last sound Jelka ever heard.